KIDNAPPED AT CHRISTMAS

The Kidnap Club

Samantha Holt

Helstone Press

CHAPTER ONE

Millie Strong did not have time for this.

She had a crate of fabric to move, the new sign to hang, not to mention Lady Hester's ribbons needed to be delivered for her three daughters, who would inevitably use them to create hideous bonnets for Spring.

Of all the nights to be kidnapped...

She smoothed a bare thumb over the button she'd torn from her captor. Covered with fabric, likely from the front of a waistcoat. She hadn't managed to observe much when the man had snatched her from the dark streets of London except that he was much, much stronger than her and able to fling a sack over her head and bind her hands with ease.

The seat beneath her was amply cushioned and she felt no whistle of air. The sound of carriage wheels and horse hooves were muffled but that could be due to the thick cloth of the sack. Her breaths were hot and thick against the material.

A less sensible woman would panic. She would fight for breath and fall into a faint. Her heart would race and her palms would be sticky.

Millie was not that woman.

Whatever she did next, she just had to keep her wits about her. After all, this had to be a mistake. Why would someone kidnap someone like her, after all? She had no wealth to speak of and few connections, save Freya and her husband. But their friendship was hardly blazed across the scandal sheets and if someone wanted to ransom anyone, it would make far more sense to snatch Freya herself than Millie.

She closed her eyes against the fabric and dropped her head to the cushion at her side. She really, *really* did not have time for this. She was meant to meet with a new girl tomorrow. With any luck, she would help Millie with the increased workload once the new haberdashery opened. She certainly needed the aid; she could not manage it all once the bigger shop opened on Fleet Street. She'd never been one to shy away from a challenge but why she'd decided Christmas was the perfect time to move to a better address, she did not know.

Of course, none of it would matter if she did not escape her captor, whoever the devil the blaggard was.

Shifting on the seat, she shook her head experimentally. The weight of the sack shifted, chafing her skin. Her hands were bound in front of her, tight but not overly so, enabling her to sit as though she was simply having a leisurely ride.

She frowned.

Which she could well be in a vehicle such as this. She reached out with her bound hands and established the size of the vehicle. The fact it was closed, combined with what felt to be a needle-work design cushion beneath her, the thick tufts of what had to be ornate patterns teasing her fingers, led her to believe this carriage belonged to some-one who either worked for someone wealthy or was wealthy themselves.

This just had to be a mistake. She was no one, nothing. All she had to offer were her callused fingertips and an eye for fabric. If someone wanted something from her, all they needed to do was ask. She could never turn down work—it was one of the things her friends hated most about her.

Will you not even cease at Christmas time? they would say.

How could she? It was her busiest time of year and with Freya marrying an earl and recommend-ing her shop to new friends, her already popular business had grown exponentially. Every paid job was important, no matter how big or small. So long as the work continued to come in, she would never go hungry or be cold again.

Well, with the exception of now.

The binding around her wrist could be partially to blame for the tingling feeling in her fingers but the wretched man had not even allowed her time to slip on her gloves. The gall of it all. Why stuff her in a luxurious carriage only to let her freeze?

The seat beneath her jolted and she set her feet firm to stop from spilling to the floor. They had to be going at quite a pace, which she supposed was to be expected, considering the driver had just snatched someone off the streets. She only hoped they did not have an accident.

Or...perhaps that would work in her favor. Though not if something happened whilst she was bound like this.

Leaning as far forward as she could, she shook like a wet dog. The sack slipped a little, then some more. Huffing, she repeated the action until the sack finally dropped to the floor. Her hair wild about her, her skin tingling from the chafing, she straightened and gave herself a moment to take in her surroundings.

The interior was dark but little flashes of light from outside offered glimpses of the ornate cushions and fabric-covered interior. The curtains were drawn, offering her no chance to glimpse her kidnapper.

"Blast," she muttered to herself, drawing in a clear breath of air and savoring it far more than she should. Ultimately, her hands were still bound.

Shifting sideways and gripping the door handle between both hands did not offer much hope either. She rattled the handle vigorously but to no avail. The man must have secured it from the outside. She briefly debated slamming a shoulder against it or even thrusting her fists through the glass, but it only offered her new problems—most likely broken knuckles and a damaged arm—but also the trouble of exiting a carriage travelling at high speeds.

She sank onto the cushions and eased out a long breath. There was nothing to do but wait. Wait and tell her captor this was all a mistake, and she should be released immediately.

That and try to slip the hat pin from her hair. If reasoning did not work, then she would have to resort to violence. She didn't like violence—she'd seen far too much of it growing up in London—but she had customers relying on her.

She would do whatever was needed to escape.

***

Only when he spotted the shadowy outline of the gamekeeper's cottage did Gabriel ease his grip on the reins. He had the woman. He had a place to stow her.

And no one had seen a thing.

He guided the horses to the rear of the stone building. It had been years since anyone used the cottage and given it was on acres of private land, the chances of anyone spotting the carriage were remote, but the cottage shielded it from the view of anyone coming up over the hill. Of course, they'd be setting foot on private land and in more trouble than he would be if anyone discovered him — however, he did not wish to make this situation any more complicated than it already was.

Or any more grim.

Miss Strong's scream as he shoved the flour sack over her head still rang in his ears. He stretched his mouth into a dour line and touched his aching side where the scars panged after their tussle. The woman didn't look like much—tall but slender. She fought like a damned hellcat, though. Strong by name, strong by nature.

He shook his head as he approached the carriage. He needed to go back to thinking of her as 'the woman.' Far easier for him to remain emotionless about this whole terrible matter. The horses could be stabled once he had *the woman* locked in the cottage. Easing the bolt slowly across the door, he eyed the tiny gap between the curtains but could see little. With any luck, the journey had tamed her. She couldn't do much with bound hands and a sack over her head anyway and, by rights, she should be terrified of him.

He smirked to himself. If she saw him, she would certainly be terrified of him. But there was a reason for the sack. Even the mask he wore across his eyes could not disguise who he was.

The door swung open abruptly, smacking against the side of the carriage so hard, he swore he heard wood splinter. From the dark recesses, a wild, snarling beast emerged and flung itself upon him, knocking him back several steps. Claws swiped his face, gouging his cheek.

He grabbed her wrists, no longer bound by rope, and prevented her from swiping again. Her eyes were white and wide in the meagre moonlight, her pale hair a halo of curls about her. Where the damned sack had gone, he did not know, but he didn't get much time to debate it before she lunged again and brought a knee up to his groin.

She missed. Barely. But it still hurt the inside of his thigh like the devil. For a woman who looked like she needed several decent meals, she had more strength than he realized.

She ripped her wrists from his grip and spun away. He grabbed the back of her cape, and she gave a strangled cry when he used it to haul her back. The cape slipped from his fingers as she fought him and she tumbled forward, falling hard upon the ground. The late hour meant frost had already begun to form and he winced as she made a sound of anguish.

With a sigh, he steeled himself to her noises and grabbed the back of an arm with the intent of hauling her up. Instead, she lashed out, her foot connecting with his shin before she lunged forward, bringing him to his knees. She swung back with an elbow which he dodged.

"Stay still, damn it." he ordered with a growl.

To his surprise, she froze for a moment, if only out of shock at the sound of his voice. He knew how it was—graveled and ugly—the perfect voice for a heartless kidnapper. Apparently, it didn't frighten her enough to make her stop for long. She scrabbled forward on her hands and knees, forcing him to follow her movements until he could grab her and flip her over, pinning her with his body. She continued to fight him, wriggling against his weight, squirming her legs in every direction and swinging her arms back and forth in his hold.

"Get off me, you trout-faced frogspawn."

Well, he'd been called a few things in his time but that was new.

"Stay still," he repeated.

"Never." Her struggles started anew.

"Damn it." He pressed hard upon her wrists, bringing them up above her and forcing them into the cold dirt and grass. It left her vulnerable and open to him. He heard her gasp of pain and winced.

He had to do this. *This is for Emma, remember?*

"I do not want to hurt you, but I will if I must," he told her through gritted teeth. He pressed harder upon her wrists.

God, why would she not cease fighting? Did she *want* him to hurt her?

With a frustrated gasp, she sagged, her arms limp. He took the opportunity to take a deep breath of cool night air and question how the hell he'd ended up in this situation. Her lithe body beneath his brought back memories of days long ago when he'd enjoyed the company of a woman.

Now he was bloody kidnapping one.

Though, she was quite attractive...

She moved abruptly, unfurling her fist, and jamming something sharp into his arm. He didn't even feel the pain, so great was his surprise. He glanced at the end of the hat pin, the tiny, balled end glinting mockingly in the moonlight.

"Pock-marked, weasel-toed wretch," she spat at him.

"Right. That's it." He pinned her wrists back down with one hand. He'd tried to be gentle, but he did not have time to be wrestling with his captive in the dirt. Wrenching the hat pin from his shoulder, he tossed it far away and hauled her up with both hands. She struggled in vain, her cape coming loose from her shoulders and falling to the ground as he lifted her over his shoulder and shoved open the cottage door with a boot.

The sooner this was all over, the better.

CHAPTER TWO

Bed ropes creaked as he flung her down. Millie held back a cry. Tomorrow, she would be black and blue from the tussle on the ground. Whoever this masked man was, he was ridiculously strong. And she had met many muscular men—men who fought for a living or hauled boxes at the docks or tugged ropes on the ships—but she never recalled any of them looking as strong as her captor.

Of course, none of them had been pressed atop her, practically crushing the breath from her.

She pushed up from the bed and flew across the room, but it was too late. The door slammed shut behind him and she heard a bolt slot into place. She slammed a palm against the door with a cry of frustration, then rattled the doorknob.

"Let me go, you liver-spotted fop!"

Her demand went unheeded, and she heard heavy footsteps move away from the door.

Drawing in a breath, Millie eyed the dark room. A shiver wracked her. It didn't look as though the building had been occupied in some time, with a barren fireplace, a tired wooden framed bed covered in a thin blanket and nothing more. She hadn't seen the other rooms of the single-story building but none of it offered her much hope.

Wind whistled through the gaps in the window frame, and she wrapped her arms about herself. If only she hadn't lost her cloak. It had been made from some beautifully warm wool Freya and Lucy had given her, and was one of her favorite items of clothing. Now it was discarded in the dirt out there somewhere and who knew when she would ever get it back again.

She snatched the blanket from the bed and tossed it about her shoulders, drawing it around her neck while she let her eyes adjust to the dim light of the room. The walls were of painted stone and cold to the touch. No one had been here to warm the bedding for years she reckoned, so her chances of being found were slim. In the window hung tattered curtains and she just spied the crescent moon trying to force its way between frosty blue clouds through filthy windows. The latch on the window refused to budge no matter how hard she pushed at it. Not that it mattered. She'd never fit through the tiny gap anyway.

Fingers of cold trailed up her spine again and she tightened her body against it. There was nothing she hated more than being cold. It reminded her of all those freezing evenings from her childhood and she swore she'd never be as cold again now she was grown and making a good living as a shopkeeper.

It seemed her captor had other ideas. Maybe he thought leaving her in such a cold room would disquiet her. Well, it would take more than a chilly room to steal the fight from her. She had not pulled herself up out of poverty to create a successful business only to have her determination quelled at the first bump in the road.

If one could consider a kidnapping a bump, that was.

He had to have the wrong person. He just had to. She might not be desperately poor anymore, but the new shop had cost her most of her savings and she had nothing to offer anyone save from a vast array of fabrics, buttons, and ribbons. If someone wanted use of those, all they had to do was pay her, and Millie suspected her captor had plenty of money. The carriage, the expensive button, and his physique all implied a man who had never gone hungry once in his life. From what little she had observed of him, his hair was neatly cut, and he smelled of soap. Hardly how one would picture a savage criminal.

Maybe if she reasoned with him...

Millie strode over to the door and slammed her palm against it several times.

"Excuse me?" she yelled, then frowned at herself. Why was she being polite to her captor? She pounded the door again and stopped when she heard footsteps. He didn't say anything.

"You have the wrong person," she told the closed door. "Just let me go and we can forget this ever happened." She waited, her thudding heart the only sound in the old cottage. Was he still there? She rattled the door with a cry of frustration. "Just let me go! Please! I...I can pay you..."

"Doubtful."

So he knew she was not wealthy. She bit down on her bottom lip. That did not bode well. It meant he might very well have intended to take her then.

"Please just let me go," she said softly. "You must have the wrong person."

"No."

Was that the answer to both of her statements or just the first?

"What could you possibly want with me?"

"Get some rest," he replied after several heartbeats of silence.

"No!" She slapped her hand against the door and gave it another rattle for good measure. "Never. And you won't rest either. I will scream and scream until you release me." She gave a wild cry in demonstration.

On the other side of the door, she swore she heard a sigh. "Scream all you want. No one will hear you."

She screamed as high-pitched and as loudly as she could while smacking both hands against the door. A thud against the other side of the door made her jolt back for a moment.

"Enough!" he demanded.

"No!"

She screamed for as long as she could, then started another. She didn't hear him move away from the door, but she suspected he was long gone by the time her voice gave out on her.

Sighing, she rubbed her throat and curled up on the bed, the blanket high around her shoulders. It did little to defeat the cold but the exertion of her fight plus an already long day at the shop made her eyelids heavy. If she rested for but a moment, then she would have the strength to fight again, she promised herself.

She woke when the bright light of dawn slipped in through the narrow window. Her throat was raw, her limbs hurt, and there was dirt under her fingernails and on her clothes, making her feel grimy and crusty. She was also covered in her beautiful wool cape.

Frowning, she eyed the closed door. Had he risked her escaping to return her cape? Had he tucked her in? And if so, who was he and why would he care, even slightly, about the welfare of his captive?

***

Gabriel eyed the boy who could be no more

than fourteen. His long, thin legs looked barely able to withstand a light breeze let alone a fast gallop to the duke's estate.

"I'm swift as a frog," the lad assured him as he tucked the letter into his pocket and grasped the reins of his mount tightly in one hand.

The messenger might be swift, but he wasn't clever. "Frogs aren't swift."

He wrinkled a freckled nose. "They are. I've never been able to catch one."

Resisting the urge to pinch the bridge of his nose, Gabriel kept the brim of his hat low over his face and handed the boy his payment. "Do not look at the letter," he ordered. "And give it to no one but the Duke of Westwick."

The messenger rolled his eyes. Somehow, Gabriel suspected he would be just as insolent even if he knew Gabriel was of rank.

"I'm the best." He puffed out shoulders that were just as scrawny as the legs.

Oh to have the confidence and arrogance of a fourteen-year-old boy.

"I'll keep your letter safe," the boy continued, "and I can get it there quicker than anyone in the country, you'll see."

"I hope so." The sooner he received a response, the sooner this whole mess could be over.

"You paid me, didn't you?" The boy tapped the jacket pocket that jangled with more coins than he had likely ever seen before. "Colin never fails a paying customer."

"Discretion is important," Gabriel said tightly.

"I know, I know." Colin waved a hand. "No one hires me because they want their business known."

"And I have paid you handsomely."

"Look, do you want this letter delivered or do you want to gossip like fishwives?"

If Gabriel had not just spent the evening wrangling a surprisingly strong and determined young woman, he might have been surprised by Colin's cheek but in the bright light of dawn, he was determined nothing would shock him now.

Gabriel hefted out a sigh. "Just be quick about it and you'll get the rest of your payment when you return."

Colin rolled his eyes and turned his mount toward the signposted village, moving off with a speed that did bode well for Gabriel. Maybe the boy's confidence was not misplaced after all.

He waited until the messenger vanished from sight before mounting his own horse and heading back to the gamekeeper's cottage. Settled against gentle hills with the vague outline of a large pond glittering in front, the ramshackle cottage offered an inviting, cozy impression in the light of day. He doubted Miss Strong would ever see it as such, but with any luck the cold, long night would have broken her spirit just enough for him to handle her until that letter was delivered.

Once he'd stabled the horse with the other at

the rear of the building, he headed around to the front, and muttered a brief curse. He stopped to pull out the simple black mask—an item he'd last used years ago at a masquerade ball. He gave a grim smile as he put it on. He'd certainly never anticipated using it in such a manner, let alone for a kidnapping.

Pausing by the bolted door, he listened for a moment. Last time he'd checked on her, she slept like the dead. He couldn't imagine having a restful night with that thin mattress and even thinner blanket but apparently she'd worn herself out enough to emit little mewling sounds as she slept. If it hadn't been for those wretched sounds, he would never have brought her the cloak.

Maybe.

But, anyway, he couldn't let her freeze to death in the middle of winter. He needed her. It simply made sense to tuck the woolen shawl about her shoulders.

He heard no shuffling or determined pacing or any other sound of the sort. She must have calmed down. He put a hand to the sturdy bolt then stilled with a tilted smile.

No, he'd underestimated her before. He wasn't going to do it again. He headed through the house, ducking under low beams and retrieving his pistol from the kitchen.

Still listening for sounds of life, he inched out the bolt, wincing at the gentle scraping sound as though it might awaken a beast. Which was not far off. She was easily as wild as the one reputed to roam the land here.

Though this wild beast was real. And crucial. She could be the key to saving his sister.

He stepped swiftly into the room to find her awake and curled upon the bed, her arms about her legs. Without being able to observe her height, she appeared petite and vulnerable. He wished to hell she didn't look at him with such pale, solemn eyes.

"Have you come to shoot me?"

"What?" He glanced at the pistol. "No. That is, unless you cause me more trouble."

"I am not the one causing trouble." She rose slowly from the bed and any idea of her being vulnerable vanished. Though a little underfed, her build wasn't as gangly as he first thought, with strong wrists and hands, and the slight rise of breasts curving the bodice of a plain cream and brown dress. Jaw set, she eyed him coolly though he caught the rapid rise and fall of her chest beneath the cloak she kept clutched about her shoulders.

"You kidnapped me," she reminded him.

He blinked and tore his gaze from where it most certainly should not be. "It was necessary."

"Necessary? How could kidnapping a shop-keeper be necessary?"

"It doesn't matter. Now do you want some food or am I going to leave you to starve?"

"Food? As if that will make all of this better?"

He ground his teeth together. "I do not care to make this better. I am simply offering you food so you do not go hungry."

"Oh how kind." He caught her glance at the pistol but too late. She raced forward, pinched her fingers into his wrist and attempted to wrestle the gun from him.

He pushed her back with ease, sending her tumbling to the floor in a puff of dirt and dust, then levelled the pistol at her. The fire in her eyes didn't diminish. Gabriel shouldn't have been grateful for the fact but rather that than tears or a trembling chin or even a cry of anguish. He did not need a reminder of the immorality behind kidnapping an innocent woman.

"You won't shoot me."

"Won't I?" He slipped a hand into his jacket pocket, retrieved a packet of powder and ripped it with practiced ease between his teeth. He eyed her while he poured the powder down the barrel and followed it with shot, ignoring the skip of his pulse.

"Why take me only to kill me? It makes no sense." Her gaze flicked back and forth between him and the door.

He took a step back and slammed it shut with the boot of his heel. Uncertainty flickered across her expression, and her gaze latched onto the end of his pistol.

"You won't kill me," she repeated, but a tremor slipped from generous lips, removing the confidence in her tone. "Anyway, I am just a shopkeeper. What possible use can I be to you?"

"Yes," he intoned. "Only a shopkeeper. And, therefore entirely disposable."

Her dark gaze hardened. He almost regretted the words. No doubt given her poor circumstances, she was used to being thought of as disposable. He knew the feeling all too well—and he'd had privilege. How much worse it must have been for her.

Damn it, he did not need to be sympathizing with his captive.

"If you want to kill me, just do it." She folded her arms. "I am tired of this charade. I see no reason to hold me here."

He crouched slowly, peering at her through his mask, allowing the pistol to rest against one knee. "You will be held here until I hear word from your father."

"I have no father?" Miss Strong laughed. "You half-witted, gangrenous fool of a lout. You have the wrong woman."

Rising, Gabriel shook his head slowly. "I do not." He motioned with the pistol for her to rise and she did slowly. "Now get on the bed and I shall bring you food."

"You'll realize you are wrong soon enough," she said imperiously as she stood and inched back to sit herself with more elegance on the edge of the bed than he might expect from a woman of her rank. "Then what a fool you shall look when you have no choice but to release me."

"Or kill you."

Her gaze narrowed. "You will not. I can tell."

"You do not know me."

"Nor do you know me." Her chin lifted.

Oh yes, there was no doubting she was her father's daughter.

"I do know you, Miss Strong. I know you to be one of the many bastard children your father sired."

The smugness dropped from her expression.

"Your father, the Duke of Westwick, and the man who intends to marry my sister."

CHAPTER THREE

Millie stared at her captor for some time. A laugh threatened to burst free from her, but it was trapped by the set of his jaw – and the piercing gaze from eyes which were of interminable color, thanks to his black mask.

This man had money, of that she was certain. His build suggested the sort of exercise that did not come from hard labor. The carefully carved jaw, almost black with stubble, could only be the work of meticulous breeding.

His clothes were the most obvious sign of money. They fit as though made specifically for him —which they likely were—from the latest fabrics and fashions. He'd changed clothes at some point too—discarding what she suspected had been the waistcoat that she had torn a button from. His current brown one might not look like anything special to the untrained eye but the woven marcella fabric and golden buttons did not come cheaply.

As much as she'd like to spill out another insult, she struggled to see a man with such resources as a half-wit.

"I do not have a father," she repeated softly, lacing her fingers together. It had been her and her mother for as long as she could remember, and her mother refused to speak of her father.

"Everyone has a father."

She shook her head vigorously, feeling her hair bounce about her face. She automatically put a hand to it, however several of her pins had long since abandoned her and there was no chance of salvaging it now. She dropped her hand to the bed.

"I would think if I was the daughter of a lord, I would know about it." Her tone betrayed her uncertainty more than she would have liked.

"What do you know of your father?" He folded his arms and peered down at her.

Damn the man. She did not like the idea of him having knowledge that she did not. Being a shopkeeper left her privy to enough information to blackmail at least fifty percent of the *ton*. Not that she would, of course! But information had been a key to her success. Knowing which young debutante needed more buttons to keep a growing bump hidden or which lord stuffed his breeches enabled her to work sympathetically with each of her clients to provide them with exactly what they needed.

To imagine she did not know such a thing

galled her indeed.

"I always assumed he was a sailor on a merchant vessel. My mother says I look like him but that's about it."

He nodded. "Your nose and chin are similar."

"You're lying," she said.

She had learned long ago asking her mother about her father hurt her gravely. It seemed easier to accept he would never be in their lives and to move on, just as her mother did. They struggled for years, of course they did, but they always managed and she had the love of her mother. What more did she need?

"What reason do I have to lie?"

"You could be mad," she said. "Or you just enjoy lying. Perhaps you find it amusing to take penniless shopkeepers and lie to them about their fathers."

"Trust me, there is nothing amusing about this situation."

"Then why take me? Do you really believe this lord—who I still do not believe could be my father—would pay ransom for a child he has never met or claimed?"

His jaw twitched. "I do not want a ransom."

Millie rose slowly from the bed, put hands to hips, and met his gaze. No sign of madness at all. "Perhaps you could explain the situation to me."

His lips quirked. "And I suppose you would come along peacefully if I did."

"What do you want from this man?"

"Your father has sired a number of illegitimate children."

She suppressed a shiver at the word illegitimate. It implied so many things. Unwanted, unplanned, unloved. That was not her, though. Her mother loved her dearly and she'd found a firm place in her world and no kidnapper could convince her otherwise.

"Many of them died in childhood, several left the country to seek fortunes elsewhere. But not you." He gestured to her. "You stayed and your business grew, and you are to move into a new shop shortly."

A chill swept through her. Had he been watching her? Investigating her? She could not decide if the thought of those shadowed eyes lingering on her as she went about her business made her scared or something else—something strange and unfathomable.

"It seems you know all about me."

"You are the only child to make a success of your life."

"There are many who would not think running a haberdashery is considered a success," she pointed out.

"Your father must have helped at some point. Did he pay the lease on the shop perhaps? Or spread word of your skills?" He rubbed his jaw, "You, Miss Strong, are special, and I will use that to get what I want from your father."

Heat blazed straight up into her cheeks, lingering there and then spreading deep into her chest. She bunched her hands. If the word special was not ringing around in her mind and making her wish it was true, she might well have launched herself at him then and there.

"I paid for the lease myself," she declared through a tight jaw. "Through my own hard work." She took a step forward. "Never, ever, have I had help from anyone. Everything I have achieved I have done on my own."

He smirked. "But of course."

Indignation blazed through her. She was used to men doubting her word—she was poor, illegitimate, and the weaker sex after all—but for the first time in her life, she was unable to turn away from her anger and frustration at such an existence.

"How dare you." She thrust a finger in his face. "How dare you do this to me then have the gall to mock me?" Another step forward and she was almost toe-to-toe with him, tilting her head to meet his hard stare. "I have worked against all odds to succeed and I have done that alone. And you...you are ruining it all. You know I was due to open my new shop soon. If you have been watching me, you must know that I have been working late every night to ensure it is ready in time for Christmas. That I have been commissioned by the Duchess of Windcombe to source fabric for her drawing room and that it will be the single biggest commission I have ever had." She took a deep breath. "And that if I am trapped here, I can do none of that, and you will be responsible for ruining my business."

His mouth opened and closed.

"You…" Her breaths came so hot and hard that she could scarcely draw them. She bunched her hands into fists. "You are just a coward. A coward who skulks in the night and claims he knows all about me but does not and…and hides behind silly masks."

"That's not—"

"And I am not going to tolerate it anymore." She swiped at the mask, successfully curling fingers into the fabric, and pulling so hard the ties snapped and she stumbled back a few steps.

Millie glanced at the torn fabric, then back at the man, his expression dark, his jaw set. And her insides shriveled a little.

She might have been wrong about him.

The mask fell from her fingers and fluttered uselessly to the floor. "I—"

He whipped up the loaded pistol. "Back on the bed. Do not move. I will shoot you, I promise."

Swallowing hard, she hastened over to the bed, drawing her legs up. She kept her gaze forward and wrapped her arms about her legs and waited, her breaths harsh in her ears, unable to move a muscle.

Only when he stormed out of the room and slammed the door shut did she allow herself a long, slow exhale.

Just who was this man? And was he really a rich man playing kidnapper or did she have it all wrong? He was more dark and dangerous than she'd realized. The scar cutting across one eye, completely deforming it, and leaving him half-blind had her wondering exactly who this abductor was.

And if her supposed father ignored his demands—which she was certain he would—exactly what would he do with her?

***

This was ridiculous.

Gabriel stared at the bolted door for too long, a platter of cheese and bread in one hand and the pistol in the other.

Was he scared of a young, skinny woman?

Of course not. He slipped the pistol into the waistband of his trousers. He'd ridden into battle for God's sakes. He'd felt the heat of cannon blast on his face, the dirt spraying up about him, tasted the tang of blood, and felt the tear of shrapnel.

One quarrelsome woman was not going to be the end of him.

He paused, fingers upon the iron bolt. What if she had recognized him? His injury had been talked about upon his return from fighting in France. Few people did not know his face or at least jumped to the conclusion. *Oh yes*, they would say, *you're the viscount who stormed into battle with his men and ended up losing an eye. Pray tell, why did you not just stay behind like the rest of the officers?*

Bloody fools. He'd like to see them send a platoon of boys to their deaths.

She *migh*t have recognized him. Or she'd simply been repulsed by him, just like the previous women in his life. Either was likely indeed.

It didn't matter. He couldn't let it matter. Emma needed his aid and he'd be damned if he was going to let her suffer because he'd been an absent brother. If Miss Strong did recognize him, there was nothing he could do about it and who was going to believe her word over his? Viscounts did not go around kidnapping women.

He slid the bolt back and stepped into the room. Sunlight dappled about her hunched form. He let his lips curve. At least she was finally obeying him. He did not think she had moved a hair's breadth since he'd left to prepare food. She rested her chin upon her knees, keeping her arms tightly wound about her legs. There was no denying what a pretty picture she made, despite her dirty and worn appearance. Her profile offered a determined chin, a nose that curved gently upward and a full bottom lip currently pulled under even teeth.

Gabriel shoved down a pang he did not want to dwell on for too long and deposited the plate at the end of the bed. "Eat," he ordered.

She shook her head.

"Eat, damn it."

Her head twisted slowly to meet his gaze, her eyes narrowed. "I do not wish to."

"Eat," he bellowed, "or I shall force you to."

Her pale brows lifted. "You were threatening to shoot me not too long ago, and now you wish me to eat?"

"Fine. Don't eat." He twisted away with a huff. "I do not care either way."

"I need a chamber pot though."

He pivoted on a heel. "So you can throw it at my head? I do not think so."

"I haven't relieved myself all night. Of course I need a chamber pot."

He nodded toward the corner of the room. "Do it there."

She gasped. "That's barbaric."

"I *am* barbaric," he said, his voice low.

"I am not asking for much," she persisted.

"And I am not a fool."

She gestured about the room. "These circumstances tell me otherwise."

He paced back toward the end of the bed. "You know for a woman being held at gunpoint, you have quite the mouth on you."

"Well, for a kidnapper you are utterly useless. First you use your expensive carriage, then you do not even equip the room with a chamber pot, and you leave me unbound—" She pressed her lips together, her eyes wide.

"I can certainly address that."

"You could address the chamber pot issue first."

"And *you* could cease making demands of the man who has you at his mercy."

He folded his arms. He prayed this woman was never kidnapped by real criminals. Her mouth would get her killed within moments. He might have no intention of harming her but, at this point, he would not mind some peace and quiet. Maybe he should bind her mouth too. That would make this whole situation much more pleasant.

"I want a chamber pot!" she demanded, slapping her hands upon the mattress, causing dust to fly up and mill around in the sunlight.

It created a strangely ethereal haze around her and he blinked a few times to rid himself of a vision of her white with the sunlight behind her, silhouetting a figure he was beginning to find increasingly intriguing.

"I'm going to tie you to the bed, damn it."

"Go ahead. I do not care." Her gaze clashed with his.

Grinding his teeth together, he stared back. Apparently even his hideous face could not diminish her courage. If only he did not admire such fire. He'd fought alongside some of the bravest men he'd ever met, and he had no doubt she would be just like them, running into the cannon blasts, sword raised high.

"Fine. I'll get you a chamber pot." He released his folded arms and pointed at the food. "Now eat the damned food."

He ignored her smug look and marched out of the room. He'd spotted a spare pot in one of the other bedrooms, though he'd have to watch her carefully or he'd end up with a face full of piss and a sore head.

Indeed, it would not be the worst thing that had ever happened to him, but he could do without any more trouble from her. The sooner this was over, the sooner his sister was free of Miss Strong's father, the better.

CHAPTER FOUR

Teeth clamped together, Millie eyed the chamber pot. It was small—too small. Even if she did strike the brute of a man over the head, she doubted it would do any harm. He was too strong and most certainly too thick-skulled. The man was practically a barbarian.

She snorted. Yes, barbarian was about right. She could imagine him in simpler, more dangerous times, decked out in some sort of armor and wielding an axe, stomping his way through newly discovered lands, and laying waste to them. He had all the manners of one, and about as much intelligence as one too. Any clever man would know snatching a shopkeeper was no way to get what one wanted.

Whatever *that* was.

She gripped the cloak, drawing it as close to her chest as possible, and peered through the window. No gentle moonlight slipped in this evening, leaving the room almost pitch black. Faint outlines of the room she had come to know far too well already emerged but offered no comfort. The temperature dropped rapidly with the waning sun—not enough to freeze her to death but enough to make her uncomfortable for yet another night.

How much longer would she have to spend here? A day? More? No one would come for her, she was certain. Her mother wouldn't worry for her until Christmas Day, knowing she had so much work to do in the new shop, ensuring she could open before the lease on her old shop ended, and her customers might be confused but would hardly jump to the conclusion she had been kidnapped. Who would?

As for this supposed father of hers, he would not come for her or give her brooding captor whatever it was he wanted. After six-and-twenty years of ignoring her existence, the idea was preposterous.

Almost as preposterous as the thought that her father might be a lord. She did not have a noble bone in her body for goodness sake. Anyone who looked at her would know that. Her fingers were callused, she forgot to eat enough some days, and her inability to hold her tongue made her about as far removed from a lady as could be.

This was ridiculous.

She slipped off the bed and paced the small room a few times, the cloak billowing behind her. Waiting around for rescue would not get her back to the new shop anytime soon, and reasoning with the empty-skulled brute would not work. Millie doubted he really would kill her—would a man intent on harm really tuck her in under a cloak? Admittedly, the eye had shocked her. However, now she was used to it, she'd returned to her original conclusion—this man was no regular kidnapper and killing her was not at all part of his plan.

It still made no sense to sit around acting all powerless. She'd eaten what food he'd given her—in the end—and regained some strength. It had to be close to midnight by now and he'd be asleep surely? If she was going to do anything, she had to do it now.

She inched over to the door and tried the handle as though by some miracle he might have forgotten to lock her in.

No such luck.

Huffing, she eyed the window. It was small but then she was hardly huge. Maybe if she contorted just so...

Millie tugged and pushed, biting back a grunt of annoyance when the iron latch would not move. The thing had to be rusted shut or something.

"Blast," she muttered to herself. If she could just get to the nearest road, maybe she could signal for help or follow it to some lone inn. There had to be one nearby considering they had come by carriage.

She tapped the glass with a finger and pursed

her lips. It was old. Very old. Maybe fragile.

Undoing the cloak from around her shoulders, she wrapped the fabric around her hand, creating a wad of padding about her knuckles. A quick prayer uttered, she drew back her fist and hit the glass. A dull thud echoed about the room and a reverberation rattled through her arm. She eyed the fabric and huffed. Too thick. She unwound it a few times, drew back her fist and tried again.

Glass shattered, the sound piercing the silence of the night. Her heart gave a wild leap against her ribs, and she eyed the damage. Large splinters of glass remained set in the frame but she could pick those out. Now if she just—

"Ouch." She twisted her hand this way and that, then unbound the fabric. "Well, that is not good..."

Even in the dark, she saw the blood pooling around her hand, felt it warm her cool skin. She couldn't tell where the cut was or how bad the damage might be in the dark and amongst the welling of blood, but it stung badly now she was aware of it. She flexed her fingers and winced.

Perhaps her captor was not the only thick-skulled one here.

She jolted from her position by the window when the door slammed open, and candlelight made her blink a few times. Hair ruffled, jacket creased, the man appeared rather wild.

And worried.

Or perhaps annoyed.

"If you throw that chamber pot at me..." He paused in the doorway, took in the sight of her hand, and closed his eyes briefly. "Oh bloody hell."

Millie looked at her hand, now able to take in the damage properly. Yes. Bloody hell was about right.

***

His sister's freedom was worth all of this. It had to be.

If there was ever a moment of doubt, however, this was it. Gabriel followed the drip of blood, watching it plop to the floor. This woman was a menace.

"What were you thinking?" he demanded as he strode over, set the candle upon the mantelpiece, and snatched Miss Strong's injured hand to inspect it.

"Oh, I do not know—perhaps I was thinking I might escape from my black-hearted, soulless barbarian of a captor."

"Barbarian? I expected better."

"Better?"

"A more inventive insult," he explained as he gently unwound the fabric and turned her hand toward the candlelight. He sucked in a breath through his teeth at the same time she made a little helpless noise that tugged at the soul she claimed he did not have.

"I would..." She closed her eyes briefly while

he pried apart her fingers to inspect the gash carving through the tender flesh beneath her thumb. "I would have been more inventive had I not cut my hand on *your* glass."

He glanced at the broken window and the hole she had created. Cold, bitter air whistled in, making him shiver, despite the thickness of his coat. Even with the golden glow of the candlelight she offered a ghostly vision of pale skin and chattering teeth. Inwardly, he uttered a curse far worse than bloody hell. This woman wasn't just a menace—she was a danger to herself. If he left her in this room, she was going to freeze to death or do something idiotic like carve herself to ribbons trying to escape.

"*My* glass was intact," he pointed out. "It is you who shattered it." He dabbed away the worst of the blood. "You are lucky you did not do more damage. You could have severed a finger or been unable to use your hand ever again."

"It's not that bad."

"I have seen men unable to hold anything ever again after such injuries."

Her gaze met his. "When?"

He ignored the question. "You are as white as a lily." He scowled and urged her onto the bed with a hand to her shoulder. "And you are going to faint."

She shook her head vigorously. "I never faint. Fainting is for fine ladies." She tried to stand but he held her down with the one hand.

A smile threatened to quirk upon his lips at her

courage. If he allowed her to stand, she would wind up a boneless puddle on the floor, of that he was certain.

"Well, pretend you are a fine lady, and stay still for a few moments." He pressed the cloak to her palm and laid her other hand over it. "Press hard."

Gabriel debated his options. He hadn't been prepared for anyone other than a terrified young woman who would sit in her room and be entirely obedient. He certainly had not expected such an injury and there were no clean cloths in the cottage. There was, however, alcohol. It was old and had likely been here since the last gamekeeper passed away but it would do the job. Unfortunately, it was in the store cupboard.

"I need to clean that." He eyed her as she wavered, her lids heavy. "Do not fall asleep on me," he ordered.

"I am not tired." She yawned.

"You are not to move, do you understand? If I do not clean that, you could die from infection." He took her chin in his hand and tried not to think about how kissable that bottom lip was. What would it feel like if he drew it between his teeth and nibbled gently on it? "Millicent, do not move. I need to clean this or you will die."

"So you do know my name." she murmured, nodding vaguely.

He knew it. And he did not like having used it. It made all of this too real. Far easier to think of her as Miss Strong or maybe just 'that blasted woman.'

"But I do not know yours," she said faintly as he ducked out the room and shut the door behind him. She wouldn't be fool enough to try to slip out of the window.

Hopefully.

By the time he returned, she'd curled up on the bed, her eyes shut.

He uttered a word he never said in female company and grabbed both her shoulders, forcing her upright again. She blinked at him and the strangest little smile crossed her lips. At first he thought it was a trick but when she put a finger to his face, he realized the pain and blood loss was making her addled.

"Handsome." The word came out on a whisper.

He almost snorted. It had been years since he'd been handsome. "This is going to sting," he warned her. He removed the fabric, pulled the cork on the alcohol, and poured it liberally over her hand. She released a tiny cry and tears welled in her eyes.

His heart gave a pang but he set his jaw and concentrated on knotting his clean cravat about her hand, cinching it tightly. The powerful tang of alcohol burned his nostrils.

"You are lucky it does not need stitches," he said gruffly. "That would be far more painful."

"You are lucky," she retorted.

"How so?"

"Because if I was dead, you would have no one

to kidnap and then you would be a terrible kidnapper and you would be alone and..." She frowned. "Alone and..."

"Alone sounds rather pleasant right now." He tied the fabric. "You should keep your hand held high." He took her wrist and lifted it into the air. "Like so."

Miss Strong peered at him as though he was mad but kept her hand held aloft, somehow creating a ridiculously endearing picture. When she was not trying to injure herself or attack him, she was rather appealing.

A gust of frigid air whipped through the room and her shoulders trembled. He ran a hand over his face and sighed. Not only was she weak from blood loss and pain but she had made the room colder than ever. She really could die if he left her in here.

"You would never have fit through there."

"I might have." Her chin lifted.

Wonderful. Already, her fire was returning. Just what he needed.

Grinding his teeth together, he took her elbow and urged her to stand. "You had better come to my room. At least I can keep an eye on you there."

CHAPTER FIVE

Admittedly, the pain had left Millie a little addled. Only briefly, though. Not addled enough to ignore that this was her chance. She snatched her cloak in one hand and allowed him to lead her by the elbow toward a room glowing with a lit fire.

How nice for him, she thought bitterly. All snuggled up in the warmth while she practically froze to death. He might have looked at her with concern and a tenderness that one could never have expected from such a brute of a man but his heart really was black, and she would do well to remember that.

She faked a stumble once she had her bearings and when he released her elbow, she whipped around and sprinted to the door, flinging it open and barreling out into the night. Pretending to be fatigued had worked well. Her captor hadn't been ready for her to flee at all. The bitter cold bit her face and she flung her cloak about her shoulders.

Behind her, she heard a curse and he bellowed her name into the night, sending a shiver down her spine.

"Millicent!"

But she was fast and she suspected he could not outrun her. His muscular build would make him slower and she'd always been speedy. Such a skill had served her well when darting between market stalls having stolen bread or vegetables just so she and her mother could eat that night. Of course, she would never do such a thing now but the ability had never left her. Living as an unmarried woman in London was not without its dangers.

A kidnapping, however, was not something she could have predicted.

She ran blindly across the fields, stumbling upon the uneven ground but never stopping. Her breaths rasped in her throat, her pulse pounded hard. She did not dare glance back in case he was behind her, looming over her like a dark, ominous shadow.

The black night offered little guidance. She kept hoping for a glimpse of lamplight or the swiftly moving lights of a carriage to guide her to a road. However, all the night offered her was the faint outlines of sloping hills and the occasional tree. She nearly toppled headlong into a shallow pond when her foot plunged into shallow water.

The icy water seeped into her boot, soaking her stockings, but her limbs were warm from running and she could not worry about whether the cold would eventually freeze her toes off right now. All she needed to do was escape.

When she finally paused to take a breath, bending double to take down gulps of air, she could not even see the lights of the cottage anymore. Nor could she hear his footsteps or any curses bellowed into the night. Hands to her hips, she peered around then up at the starless sky. The night was deathly quiet, with only the slightest whistle of wind. No creatures wanted to brave such a harsh night and she did not blame them.

Only a fool would be out on these moors at this time of night.

And that fool was her.

Oh Lord, she might well have made the wrong decision. But what was better? Be at the mercy of that man or at the mercy of these barren lands?

She considered the warm fire, the way he had bound her hand so tenderly, his slightly calloused hands brushing her own very calloused ones, and the way his brow furrowed with concern. Was she really wishing she was with him now?

No. This would not do. Moving more slowly, she gripped her cloak about her, and took careful stomping steps in what she hoped was a straight line. Eventually she would come upon a road or a building or something surely? How vast could these lands be anyway?

Her hand throbbed as though to poke at her confidence. She tutted when her imagination conjured images of beasts prowling the moors or ghosts following behind her or even her frozen body being discovered months later and her poor mother...

"No!" She marched on aggressively, head low against the increasing wind as she made her way up the brow of a hill. "He's a madman. He has to be," she told herself. "Do not forget he thinks you're a daughter of a lord." She laughed aloud. "As if a shopkeeper like me has any airs."

The top of the hill offered no hope. It seemed as though all she could see was black. Black grass, black hills, blacker outlines of hills, and maybe the faintest hint of the darkest blue for the sky. But what other choice did she have? She did not imagine she could find her way back to the cottage and she'd rather freeze to death than crawl back to him and beg for a seat by his fire. She simply had to continue on.

Millie wasn't certain how long she'd walked for, nor how much distance she might have covered. However, the heat from her sprint had long since vanished, leaving her teeth chattering and her wet foot decidedly numb. Her thick cloak might as well be made from satin for all the good it did her. Her ears passed cold, becoming aching and agonizingly cold. Soon she wouldn't be certain they still existed. She alternated tucking one hand inside her cloak, then the other, just to keep them from going completely numb. Those bits that were not numb hurt.

And her mind...it could be fatigue, it could be hunger, it could be from the loss of blood, but her mind was scattered and thick, as though someone had filled it full of wool. Her lids were heavy and she nearly spilled over several times, throwing her hands wide at the last minute to prevent herself from falling completely.

It was no good. She needed to rest.

Finding a flat and dry spot, she curled up on her side, and pulled her cloak tightly about her. She would close her eyes for only a few moments before continuing on—far away from that barbarian.

***

There were a few scenarios Gabriel had considered when he'd decided to free his sister from the Duke Westwick's clutches. Taking his illegitimate daughter had been a wild gamble and if he did not hear from her father via the messenger boy soon, he'd conclude it had failed. He had not, however, expected the bloody woman to try to kill herself on the moors.

He scanned the land as the mist burnt off with the early morning sun, spying nothing but wiry shrubs. Of course, he could have ridden right past her last night and not known it. The faint gray cast of morning offered a better view of the area surrounding the cottage and he'd covered some distance on horseback.

Bloody, damned foolish woman. If he did not already have a sprinkling of gray hairs at his temples, he'd blame her for them. At this rate, she was going to age him by several years.

She had to be alive. If only to torment him for a while longer. She just had to be.

He urged the horse back around. Even with legs as fast as hers, he doubted she would have managed to travel much farther. His breath misted in front of his face and frost clung to the ground, glinting in the sunlight. The cold would have sapped her energy too quickly and she was still weak from the cut on her hand.

Damn her spirit, damn her courage. Could she not have been the meek, mild woman he expected? No wonder she'd been furious he implied her father helped her get to where she was now. He'd been entirely wrong that Westwick might actually care for her. A woman willing to risk death for her freedom would do all she could to claw her way up from the shame of being born to an unwed mother.

Which meant his plan was likely going to fail, and his sister would never be free.

He shook his head. There was no sense in thinking about that yet. First, he needed to find Miss Strong and ensure she was still alive, if only to cause him more problems.

He headed back toward the cottage. If he

worked his way back out in circles from the building, he'd have a better chance of finding her. The chances of her walking in a straight line in the dark were slim. The odds were, she travelled less distance than she'd have liked.

His search plans weren't needed, though. He came upon her about a mile from the cottage, curled upon the ground, a far too small bundle of dark wool. Breath held, he dismounted the horse, tore off a glove and pressed fingers to her neck, aware his hand trembled. Icy to the touch, he allowed himself a breath when he felt the faint flicker of a pulse and she stirred. When he eased her into his arms, she murmured something nonsensical and pressed a cold nose into his throat.

A pang struck him, so painful and deep, it made him nauseated. Much longer out here and she'd have died.

He'd nearly killed her.

Once he'd settled her on the horse and climbed up, he arranged her in his lap. She moved with him but barely seemed aware of his presence, her eyes firmly shut. Keeping his arms wrapped about her, he made his way back to the cottage and hoped the fire still offered a few warm embers when they arrived.

Gabriel glanced at her ashen face, pale lashes fanned across her cheeks. "Do not die," he urged softly. "You still have many more insults to shout at me."

She shifted in response, burrowing her face into his chest, and creating that awful sensation in his gut. It had been years since a woman had touched him, let alone curled up against him.

He smiled wryly. What a fool he was, responding to the touch of a half-frozen woman.

He dismounted outside the cottage and hauled her down into his arms, quickly looping the reins of his mount around the nearby post for now. She remained resting against his chest with few signs of life apart from the slight stirring when he set her down on the chair in front of the fire. A few embers blazed and he quickly stoked it back to life. Perhaps he was not entirely cursed, though if he did not warm her soon, she could still ail, and he'd have even more trouble on his hands.

A smirk lingered on his face. It was hard to imagine this scrawny, pale woman could cause so much hassle, especially when folded into a tiny ball. He glanced at her features, the determined chin tucked away under the wool of her cloak, those flashing eyes safely closed. As crazed as she might be, she had more courage than half the officers he'd fought with in the war.

After retrieving a blanket and wrapping it about her, he remained crouched at her side, and took her frozen fingers between his, rubbing them between both hands, being careful to avoid her injury. He watched for signs of life, for those eyes to snap open and for her to call him a toad or a louse or some other irritating or ugly creature. At this point, he'd be happy to hear such words spilling from her lips. Anything would be better than this pale, lackluster woman in front of him.

He touched her cheek and tried not to think about how soft her face was compared to his own. Marred with scars on one half, and covered in bristle that was starting to itch on the other, could they be more contrasted?

The fire blazed, prickling through his clothing, yet she remained motionless. Cursing under his breath, he rose, lifted her into his hold and sat with her in his lap. He rubbed her fingers again, then moved up her arms and her back before drawing her tight to him. She made a small sound and he felt the tightness around his gut loosen a little.

After what seemed liked hours but might have been minutes, her lashes fluttered open. She peered up at him blearily for some time before murmuring, "Barbarian."

He couldn't help the smile flickering on his lips.

She shifted in his hold, curled her fingers into the lapel of his jacket, and released a long sigh. When her pale gaze met his, he knew what he was going to do. He did not know why and he certainly knew he shouldn't.

But his gaze dropped to her lips regardless, and when her chin tilted, he had no choice.

He lowered his mouth to hers.

CHAPTER SIX

I t had been a long time since she'd last been kissed.

Though comparing this kiss to any other was rather like comparing hot to cold or wet to dry. Millie had never experienced anything like this.

His mouth was soft, gentle, exploratory. He sought permission and she gave it—for some unknown reason she gave it.

She'd blame her night on the moors. It was as good an excuse as anything else. She wanted warmth and comfort and what better place to get it than in the arms of this astonishingly gentle man.

Who was also her captor.

She wouldn't ponder that bit for too long.

Reaching out, she curled trembling fingers around his neck and eased up into the kiss. His fingers flexed around her back and his other hand pressed into her arm. She grew aware of the firmness of his thighs and how broad he was, how easily he held her in his warm, delicious embrace. When she opened her mouth to him and his tongue met hers, she forgot anything other than sensation. The misery of the night vanished, leaving her feeling warm and liquid, and desperate for more.

When she shifted, leaning her breasts into his chest, and making a little noise, he stilled. He didn't tear away immediately but he eased the kiss, ensuring she knew it was over. The madness was done.

And now she was left with a sense of shame, her cheeks blazing hot in contrast with the rest of her still cold body. His dark brown gaze searched hers and she forgot the missing eye or the scars down one side of his face. It was hard to think of him as some kind of brute when he held her so tenderly and kissed like a man exploring a newly discovered wonder.

"W-why did you do that?" she asked, her voice a tremulous whisper. "You're a barbarian."

The words did not hold as much strength as she would have liked. In truth, she was struggling to see him as a vicious captor still, not when he tended to her so diligently. This man had a story—she just knew it—and fool that she was, she wanted to understand it.

"A barbarian," he repeated, a half-smile upon his lips. "Yes, I know." He looked her over but there was no malice or annoyance in his expression. "If I leave you here, can I trust you not to try to run away again? You need clean bandages."

She twisted her hand to peer at the grubby fabric about her hand. She didn't think she had the strength to run again let alone the willpower, nor did she believe this man intended to hurt her.

"I'll stay," she vowed.

He narrowed his gaze at her then eased her off his lap, lifting her and setting her upon the chair on which he just sat. The fire blazed and crackled, beckoning her to lean forward and warm her hands. It was the first time she'd felt warm in days and she did not think she would be able to resist staying here for hours, even if she did want to run. Her captor gave her one last glance then left the room.

She studied the modest parlor room while he was gone. Save for the fire, it did not offer much more comfort than the bedroom he'd kept her locked in. He must have slept on the chair at night and there was something strangely appealing about the image of him sitting awake at night, watching her door, wondering about her. Had he thought about kissing her before? Did he consider her pretty?

Millie shook her head at herself. Now was most certainly not the time for vanity and considering her hair had fallen from its chignon long ago and her clothes were grimy and smelled of dirt and damp, she doubted there was much that was pretty about her. Why he had kissed her was anyone's guess and it was ridiculous to even ponder it and why she had kissed him was quite enough story, and one she would have to work out on her own.

He returned with another cravat, and he kneeled in front of her to unwrap her hand. "My last cravat," he warned her as he tenderly cleaned her hand. "Try not to dirty this one too."

She hissed and tugged her hand away when he struck a particularly tender part of it.

"Forgive me," he murmured.

Frowning, Millie studied him. A curling dark lock spilled over his forehead and the bristle on his jaw had grown thicker and darker. Even with the scars, there was no doubting how handsome he was. Before his injury, he must have broken dozens of hearts.

"How did that happen?" She gestured to his face.

He glanced up as he wound the cloth around her palm. "War," he said simply.

Well, she supposed that explained a lot. If he had been a soldier, he must have witnessed some awful sights. Perhaps before going to war he had been some rakish charmer, and the experience had left him this strange mix of brooding and gentlemanly behavior. There were several men where she and her mother lived who had gone off to war and come back entirely different people.

"You know, you could have left me to die."

"I could have," he agreed, not meeting her gaze.

"I do not think you are a practiced kidnapper."

"Is this where you call me an addle-brained, warty toad-face?"

"There must be a reason you are doing this."

He fixed her with a firm look. "Obviously."

"And what is it? What do you want from this duke if it is not money? Because fabrics like this do not come cheaply," she nodded to the cravat, "and you speak far too eloquently to be an uneducated man. Despite everything, I do not believe you are addle-brained."

His jaw ticked as he tied the fabric into a complex knot. Her heart beat hard and Millie hadn't realized how much she depended on this answer. *Please do not let this be about money.* She could not bear it if she was wrong about him, she simply couldn't.

After too many painful heartbeats, he looked at her and said, "He has my sister."

***

There were many reasons not to tell Miss Strong why Gabriel had decided to kidnap her.

A logical man—a man who had not just kissed the woman he'd kidnapped—would have remained quiet. Perhaps it was because he hadn't kissed a woman in an age or because of how soft her lips were.

Or perhaps it was simply because of *her*.

The courage and fortitude this woman showed rivalled that of some of the soldiers he'd fought with and it was impossible not to admire it. All it took was one sweet, delicious kiss from her, one touch from her hands, one brief feel of her body, and here he was confessing things she had no business knowing.

"He has your sister?" Miss Strong repeated. "Like how you have me?"

He released her hand, setting it gently into her lap and ignoring the aching need to touch her again, even if it was just the briefest caress of her fingers. Damn and blast. If he had to kiss her could she not at least stare at him like she loathed him instead of with those big, curious eyes? Could she not have shoved him away and fled from him rather than lifting her chin in invitation and folding her slender body into his?

Rubbing a hand across his rough jaw, he eased out a breath. "They are engaged."

She blinked a few times. "Well, that is not at all like me." Her brow furrowed. "You put me through this because of a mere engagement? You took me, frightened me, had me freeze half to death because you do not like your sister's fiancé?"

He shoved himself up to standing. "She does not like him either," he snapped.

"Can she not simply end the engagement? There will be no scandal upon her if she does."

"It is not as easy as that," he said tightly, a fist curled at his side as he recalled the mocking words of Westwick, the pure delight in his expression when he knew he had Gabriel and his sister precisely where he wanted them. He rose and paced to the window. Miss Strong wasn't wrong. He'd put her through an experience that would break most women.

Not her, though. Oh no. This fool of a woman came up behind him, put a hand to his arm, and forced him to eye her resolute stance.

"What has this man—my supposed father—done that makes you act with such desperation?"

He smirked. But of course she saw his desperation. Only a fool would behave as he had, not only taking a woman from the streets, but giving in to every temptation to be anything other than a ruthless kidnapper to her.

And kissing her, naturally.

To look at him, anyone would think he *was* a ruthless man—a killer perhaps. It was not far from the truth. He had the blood of many men on his hands. Why could he not feel that cool calculation when deciding if it was he or his foe who survived that day when with her?

"He knows things of us—things that would ruin us both." He narrowed his gaze at her. "Do you really know nothing of your father? Have you never been curious?"

She frowned. "Of course not. Why would I say otherwise?"

"I find it hard to believe you are not curious."

"I do not have the time or resources to be curious. My mother did not wish to speak of him and what would I do to even find him?" Her frown deepened. "I am not even certain how you discovered me..." she paused a moment before adding, "not that I am convinced you are correct, though," in an arch tone.

"I do have resources," he said. "And I am correct."

"People would think I am mad if I told them I am the daughter of a lord—even if a bastard one."

He flinched. Bastard didn't do her justice. Westwick hadn't done her justice. Gabriel knew enough of Miss Strong to know she brought her and her mother up from poverty and had no doubt she would continue to thrive in a world that wasn't easy for women, let alone unconnected, poor ones. Had she been looked after and given the benefits of her father claiming her, she'd have thrived tenfold.

Though, given the nature of her father, perhaps it was best she had never known him. There were better fathers who had ruined many a child.

"After the engagement, I had several investigators dig into Westwick's past."

"So you could have some information on him? Like he does you?"

"Indeed." And there probably was some—perhaps worse than what Westwick knew of him and his sister—but it was buried deep, so deep he had yet to discover it.

The worst he had encountered was a string of illegitimate children and for many men of his rank, that was sadly not unusual. Gabriel could not imagine being blessed with a child and wishing to ignore its existence.

"So you discovered me or so you say."

"You are his daughter. Your mother worked briefly in his household and my investigator found the midwife who attended your birth. It was no secret that it was Westwick who sired you."

Her eyes flashed. "Perhaps you should have left secrets where they were."

He shrugged. "I needed information and the story of your birth was part of that."

"How charming." She pursed her lips. "You really are certain of this are you not?"

"Indeed."

She put fingers to her mouth, reminding him of how long it had been since he had tasted her lips.

Not that he would be tasting them again.

"My mother did not wish to speak of my father ever."

"She lost her job and I highly doubt Westwick was kind about it. He's a ruthless bastard."

"So you say, but surely many an unhappy match is made with men of his rank? Will your sister not have protection and wealth?"

"I can protect and look after my sister well enough," he said tightly.

"Because you are rich."

"Enough."

"Because you are..." She eyed him for a few

moments and shook her head. "No. You cannot be titled."

He glanced at the floor then looked back at her to see her eyes widen. He shouldn't be confessing as much but at this point, it hardly seemed to matter.

"Actually I am."

Miss Strong wavered and he hastened forward to take her arm. "Please tell me you are not going to faint."

She twisted to eye him. "Never!"

She collapsed into his hold.

***

Millie straightened as soon as she felt his strong arms curl about her, staggering a few steps to the right and then one to the left. A hand to her head, she drew in a deep breath, and willed her spotty vision to clear.

Her captor waited, hands outstretched and shadowing her movements.

She narrowed her gaze at him. "That was not a faint."

An eyebrow arched. "It looked very much like one to me."

She inhaled deeply. "What sort of a lord are you?"

"Only the lowliest." He gave a shrug.

"A viscount?" She laughed when he nodded. No matter how often she interacted with the world of the nobility, she would never understand him. She might as well have called him a feather-brained, stuffed breeches wearing, pox-ridden fly. "Why on earth would you do this yourself?" She gestured about the room. "Why would you not hire someone?"

"I did not want anyone else involved," he said tightly.

"I imagine you decided if it was discovered that you had taken me, no one would much care."

"Actually, I did not."

"Piffle."

The *viscount* stepped closer to her. "I did not want anyone else involved in this matter. It is too sensitive. Besides, if one wants a job done well, one should perform it oneself."

She made a small sound of agreement and regretted it. Indeed, she had found that out long ago when she opened her first shop. It was far easier to do things oneself than rely on hired help. But now she made it seem as though she agreed to this madcap plan of his.

Shifting her hands to her waist, she tilted her head. "How am I to believe you?"

"Do you really believe I wish to tell you such things, Miss Strong?"

"What is your title then? Your full title?"

He hesitated.

"Well?" she demanded. Perhaps if he gave her his full name she'd recognize it.

"Lord Gabriel Vincent, Viscount Thornbury."

Gabriel. But of course a man with such a dark

countenance would be named after an angel. She met his steady gaze, searching his eyes or expression for signs of lies. This man had snatched her from the streets and thought through a plan of keeping her in the middle of nowhere. He could be lying, though she could not fathom why. Perhaps he thought she would bow to his will because of his rank? But if he was going to lie about his rank, why not make it obvious in the first place? And why not call himself a duke—a man with almost as much power as a king?

"I am not calling you 'my lord,'" she said and then felt ridiculous.

This whole scenario was beyond absurd. Here she was conversing with her captor as though they were having light tea and finding out about one another.

"I rather liked Barbarian." A faint smile flickered upon his lips and she thought it might turn into a full one but the pounding of horse hooves distracted him, pulling his mouth into a tight line.

Millie highly doubted anyone was here to rescue her. Yes, someone would notice she was gone soon enough, however, how would they even fathom where she was? Or that she had been taken? And who in their right mind would conclude she had been kidnapped?

He peered out of the window, pointed his finger and ordered her to 'stay.'

She ignored him and marched after him, following him outside to meet the rider. He glanced at her and looked to the sky. "What did I say?"

"I *am* staying." She stomped both feet in place as a demonstration.

The young boy on horseback gave her a confused look, then with an apologetic look handed Gabriel a bound letter. "He refused to even take it. I insisted but the butler sent me away."

Gabriel cursed under his breath in language she'd never heard a gentleman use before. The concern etching his brow caught on her heart, tugging it tight. Why she should even care if he was upset she did not know. Perhaps it was his patent love for his sister or the fact that this man was not at all the barbaric kidnapper she thought him to be.

Either way, she would have to be cautious. Everyone always said she had a soft heart underneath her harder exterior. The number of assistants she'd hired who turned out to be terrible or unreliable or had even stolen from her was preposterous but she could not help herself—if someone needed aid and it was in her power to offer it, she always would.

"What will you do now?" she asked him.

"Another letter." He went to march inside and then paused in front of her. "This means he does not know I have you."

"You think I would be offended if he does not care?" She tried to search for some sort of pang of pain but came up wanting. She didn't know who her father was, still was not convinced she was even related to this man, and had a loving mother who had raised her in dire circumstances with more care and kindness than many in more privileged positions.

"I—" He huffed out a breath and headed inside, ducking under the low doorway.

Millie followed him. "What will you say?"

"Perhaps if I send the boy back to him, he shall see the urgency of the letter." He whipped out a piece of paper from a stack piled neatly on a dusty table in the kitchen and leaned over it hastily to scrawl something. She peered over his shoulder but he folded the letter swiftly and intricately so no one could access the letter with ease. Then he wrote his name on the outside for Westwick's attention.

"If someone else reads that, that is proof you have kidnaped me," she reminded him.

"I know."

"It is a great risk."

He lifted his brows. "Why should you care?"

Yes, why should she care? If someone discovered her fate, she would be rescued.

"I must free my sister from him."

"Why?" she demanded. "What is so awful about this man that she cannot marry him? Surely marrying a duke would…" She frowned and waved a hand. "Is that not the sort of match noble people want?"

"Not," he said, the veins in his neck pulsing, "after the way he treated my sister and *not* when he ensured I killed another man for his sins."

***

Gabriel met Miss Strong's gaze. Her mouth formed an 'O,' her eyes were wide. She could not be feeling any more horror, than he, however.

This carefully hatched plan had gone from one disaster to the next. Perhaps she was right about him, perhaps he was an addled-brained, six-toed oaf or whatever it was she called him. First, she'd been injured, then she escaped and nearly died, and then he'd damned well kissed her.

Not just any kiss either. It was the sort of kiss men fought over, and he knew too much about fighting.

Oh and now he had confessed his deepest, darkest secret, not to mention given over information on his sister that no one else knew. He could blame his frustration over Westwick dismissing his letter. He could also blame how bloody exhausting it was ensuring Miss Strong did not cause herself more harm.

However, it was more than likely it was simply *her* causing his loose tongue. Those eyes, her demanding tone, how she'd felt in his arms—it all combined to a strange, truth-making concoction that had him spilling his secrets.

"Forget I said that," he said abruptly.

"Oh no." She shook her head vigorously. "You

cannot confess to such a thing and tell me to forget it." Gaze narrowed, she planted herself firmly in front of him, blocking his exit to the room.

Of course, he could manhandle her. After all, it wasn't as though he had not snatched her and thrown her over his shoulder or dragged her into a cold, dark room. He eyed the smudges under her eyes, the binding about her hand, and the wild, fair hair now flowing about her shoulders. What had become of him? Had desperation made him deranged? He pressed his teeth together.

She hadn't been wrong to call him a barbarian. And now he could not bring himself to continue to behave so.

Easing a breath out between his teeth, he rubbed a hand over his rough jaw. "Do you know anything at all of your father?"

"We already had this conversation, you know I do not, and I am not at all convinced this duke you speak of really is my father."

"You must have heard of him, surely? He is a powerful man."

She cocked her head. "I send fabrics to many big households but a duke would hardly deign to set foot in a haberdashery and I have no recollection of his name in my records."

Somehow, he imagined Miss Strong would know every little element of her business, down to which customer purchased a blue ribbon on Wednesday last. He'd been thoroughly mistaken that her father might have helped her financially in some way. She'd survived and thrived on utter determination and hard work.

He could not help but admire it. His investigations had revealed few of Duke Westwick's children managed as much, their mothers thrown from his household or utterly shamed from society, leaving the bastard children with nothing. One of them could not even be found—the first known lover of Westwicks's. Gabriel dreaded to think what might have happened to her.

"He...took advantage of my sister some years ago."

"Advantage?" Her face paled. "You mean..."

"She did not consent to his attentions." Heat bubbled under his skin in an instant when he thought on his sister's sobbed confession, of how she blamed herself.

"Oh Lord..."

"She bore a child from that—a girl named Lydia. I protected her and ensured it was never known—our parents are dead, you see—and in a way, I am grateful. My mother would never have survived knowing such a fact, but Westwick knew. In fact, he ensured another man took the blame. My sister refused to name her attacker for a time and..." He shook his head. "Damn it, Strong, why do you even want to know all this?"

"You have rather involved me in this, have you not?" A tiny smile flickered on her lips. "Besides, if he really is my father, I deserve to know his true nature, and your sister's child would be related to me, would it not? I think we are entangled now."

Gabriel met her firm gaze. He only had himself to blame, to be certain, and he could not stand the thought of her somehow getting tangled with her father without knowing the sort of man he was. Her being his daughter would not protect her from his machinations.

"He demanded Emma's hand not two months ago, after his mourning period from his previous wife passed."

"Well, he sounds charming."

"It is not uncommon for rich men to seek a wife with haste—a mother for his children—that kind of thing. But his interest in my sister has little to do with her ability to be a mother—his heirs are all but grown. The fact is, she is a beautiful young woman and will have others ask for her hand soon enough. He wishes to possess her so no one else can."

A little shudder wracked her shoulders. "Possess," she repeated. "As though she is an object and not a person in her own right."

"Men like Westwick do not see women as people."

"I could not imagine having to wed the man who...who did such a thing to me."

"And neither can she. Emma has not slept since he forced her to say yes to him, and scarcely eats.

She tries to remain optimistic but I fear she will not survive a year with him."

Miss Strong tucked her bottom lip under her teeth and tapped a finger to her mouth. "It sounds awful."

"It is awful, and I will do whatever I can to protect her from him." He waved the letter. "Including being hung for kidnapping."

"I rather think your sister would not appreciate that."

"I have little choice."

"Unless..." She gave a firm nod. "Yes."

"Yes?"

"I've decided."

He scowled and searched her expression for something he'd missed. He came up wanting. "Decided what?"

Opening her hands wide, she gestured up and down herself and grinned. "You can keep me."

Gabriel lifted a brow and eyed her. Inwardly, he groaned.

CHAPTER SEVEN

G abriel, or Lord whatever it was—she'd already forgotten the lengthy title—was peering at her askance. Millie had always considered two eyes necessary to look at one as though one had lost one's mind but apparently not.

She did not much blame him. If she told the story to anyone else, they would send her to Bedlam. *Why did you not just run or beg help from the messenger boy? Why on earth did you offer your aid to the man who snatched you from the streets?*

Oh yes, why did you kiss him too?

Her friends would ask all of that of her and more, and she wouldn't have many sensible answers save from the fact that if this man he spoke of was her father, she had some sort of responsibility.

Perhaps.

More than that, it was his sister's tale that plucked at her heart. Whether Westwick was her father or not, too many women had suffered at his hands by the sounds of it. The one privilege of being poor and of no consequence was she had the freedom to choose her fate. Even her mother had such a thing. No one cared if a mere maid birthed an illegitimate child. No one even noticed.

Gabriel's sister did not have such freedoms and she pitied her.

"Your father is a dangerous man," he said tightly, still eyeing her.

She lifted her chin, refusing to give him any sign of weakness. She might have her doubts but once she made a decision, she stuck with it, regardless as to whether it was the best decision or not. A flaw and a virtue of hers sometimes.

"So now you do not wish me involved? I rather think you might have thought of that *before* kidnapping me."

His jaw twitched. "I had little choice."

"Well, now I am giving you a choice. Keep me, send word to my father, barter for your sister's freedom."

"I could just lock you away anyway."

She thrust a thumb toward the door. "And I could run now and I do not think you would stop me." She closed the gap between them and prodded his chest, trying not to think about how firm it was. "You have lost your will to fight, Gabriel, Lord so and so."

"Well, if anyone is to blame for that, it is you." He took her finger and held it firm. "What would you know about fighting anyway?"

"I am a bastard woman in a world that scarcely acknowledges my existence. I know everything about fighting."

His chest rose and fell with a deep breath. Slowly, he released her finger. "Your father would not care if he hurt you."

"I am his blood. Apparently." She shrugged. "He might not have a care for my welfare but surely he would not harm his own child?"

Gabriel's lack of response sent a chill through her. She served many high-ranking lords and ladies and she understood well the power a duke had. Clearly, this man did not use that power well. His treatment of Gabriel's sister should have been proof enough that the man would not mind stooping to any level to get what he wanted, she supposed.

"The fact that I am of no consequence would help matters surely?" she continued. "He would not consider a mere shopkeeper as a threat."

"He does not know you."

She smiled at his dry tone. "That he does not."

"I do not like it." He spoke with a grunting tone that made her think back to the idea of him being a barbarian. In some ways, it was hard to picture him being a lord. There was something basic and elemental about him, as though he should have been born in a different era, wielding a sword, and defending villages from invaders.

"You do not have to like it, and, as I said, you

brought me into this."

"I did." He stepped back, folded his arms, and peered out of the window at the waiting messenger. "What do you suggest?"

"I will wait for two more days with you. Send the letter and see if we get a response."

"Two days?"

"Your rider is fast, is he not? And I must return to London by then—my new shop must be open in plenty of time for Christmas."

"The boy will have a response by then, yes," he said reluctantly. "But if your father does not—"

"If he does not care if I am alive or dead, there is no sense in continuing this kidnap ruse, *and* I have a new shop to open before Christmas. I must return to Town as soon as possible."

"Two days then," he agreed, "then I shall return you."

The reluctance in his tone had to be from the idea of his kidnapping ruse not working and not from the thought of parting from her. It shouldn't make her stomach drop but it did. Perhaps she would put *herself* in Bedlam after all this was over...

"And then, we do whatever we can to free your sister."

"We?"

"I have some friends..." she said.

"How nice for you."

"They have certain skills. I believe they could help."

"Help?" he repeated. "I do not want anyone else knowing of this situation."

"Is that why you decided to do this yourself? To dirty your hands?"

"That and I do not trust anyone to do the job as well."

"Oh yes, you did an excellent job of kidnapping me."

"I can find some spare rope," he threatened with a slight smile upon his lips. "I never did get a chance to tie you to the bed."

Bed and the thought of his hands upon her made heat flush straight into her face. She shoved aside the strange images she had no intention of entertaining. "These friends of mine—they perform a certain service, and it is vital their actions stay secret. They will not reveal you."

At least she hoped they could help. Lucy was in Town, readying gowns for the festive season and as far as she knew Freya, who was married to the leader of this group, intended to remain near her parents for winter. She was certain once she appealed to Freya, they would want to help.

"I do not like it," he muttered.

"You do not have to but the fact is, to take on a man as powerful as Westwick, you need help." She paused. "*We* need help."

"We?" His smile was bemused. "Strong, you are really something else."

"That I am. And with the help of The Kidnap

Club, we shall free your sister. I am certain of it."

"The Kidnap Club?" he asked, brows raised.

"Yes. I'll explain…"

CHAPTER EIGHT

"**Y**ou could ride in the carriage, you know."

Millie pulled the blanket tight about her and glanced at the stone marker embedded into the frosty ground as they passed. They only had another half a mile until London. The roads grew less rutted and better maintained the closer they got but the weather did not warm with the rising sun, her breaths misting in front of her.

"I spent a rather uncomfortable journey in there if you remember," she said. "I should rather be up here. Free."

Gabriel's lips quirked though his gaze did not leave the road as he guided the carriage expertly down the tree-lined path. The only hint of civilization was a farmhouse and an abandoned plough. The roads would be busier if it were the height of the Season but at Christmastime much of the *ton* would be in the country, readying themselves for parties with friends and family and avoiding arduous winter travel.

It did not make her any less busy, though. Fabrics would need to be sent out to the big houses, various dressmakers, and there were still plenty of young women looking to trim hats with new ribbons and accoutrements. She'd lost two days to waiting around for a response from the duke.

She twined her fingers together to keep herself from tapping them against her knee. The gloves Gabriel had loaned her were too big, flopping about on the ends of her fingers, though at least they kept her hands warm which was more than could be said for the rest of her. Despite her wearing her cloak and the blanket, the bitter weather ate through the layers with ease.

The sooner she arrived at her new shop, the better. She could get warm quickly enough by setting to work.

A shiver travelled through her and she gritted her teeth against it.

"I can stop," he suggested, "and you can get warm inside."

"I told you, I prefer my freedom."

He looked to the sky. "I am hardly going to kidnap you again. As we well know, that plan did not work."

It did not. His letter had been returned again, this time opened. The contents were not of interest to Westwick. For some reason, the fact he'd actually cast his eye over the note yet sent no response gave her a tiny ache in her chest. She'd never noticed the lack of a father in her life—she did not have the time or the privilege to do so. Her and her mother were too busy trying to make a living to worry over such matters and the love of her mother was more than enough. But if there was ever a more sound rejection, this was it, and, well, no one liked rejection after all, did they?

Another shudder travelled through her, making her teeth rattle. Gabriel huffed, shifted a little then moved the reins to one hand. Millie did not comprehend what he intended until he wrapped an arm about her, drawing her tight against his side, and took the reins in the other hand again, effectively capturing her against him.

Her initial instinct was to push away but his patent strength prevented her from doing much more than wriggling slightly in his hold. Once the warmth of his body enveloped her, she could not bring herself to fight so she sank against him. Why not be comfortable and warm? He owed her as much anyway.

She looked up at him. "If the Duke of Westwick —"

"Your father," he corrected.

"My *supposed* father," she said, "is such a terrible man, there will be some information on him."

"I have investigated him as thoroughly as possible within the short time I have had. There is no doubting he is a vile excuse for a man, but a few minor scandals will not harm him."

"Once I have checked on the shop, we can go to Lucy. She'll be working no doubt and she can put us in touch with Freya."

"Explain to me who Freya is again."

"Lady Henleigh now. You would know her surely? She married the Earl of Henleigh last year."

She saw his brow furrow and it struck her how strong his jaw was from this angle, even when scattered with curling, dark hair. "I think I was invited."

"But you did not go?"

"There's something about my face that people find rather...off-putting." He smirked. "Cannot fathom what it is."

She opened her mouth and closed it. There was no denying the scar to his eye shocked one when one first spotted it, however, it did not detract from his chiseled cheekbones or his full lips. There had to be many a lady of the *ton* who would not care about such things, especially given he was titled too, yet he had already told her, in no uncertain terms, that he was not married.

"How did you get that scar?" She felt his muscles tense about her.

"I told you, war."

"So it was not the duel?"

"No."

"You have still not explained the circumstances behind that either, you know." Throughout their two days together, he stayed frustratingly quiet on this matter of the man he'd murdered for dishonoring his sister. Given duels were illegal, the information ensured Westwick had a hold over Gabriel, and Millie now knew it had been a big mistake but nothing more. One would think if he truly wanted her aid, he would divulge such details but getting Gabriel to talk freely was about as easy as ironing creases from silk.

"It is hardly something one should talk about with a lady."

"I am not a lady," she pointed out.

"You are the daughter of a duke."

She snorted. "Allegedly. And with none of the manners or refinements of one." She peered up at him. "A daughter of a duke would be thoroughly scandalized to be riding next to you like this."

He shifted his arm slightly, easing the hold upon her. "You can go back to being cold then."

"No!" She clamped her mouth shut when he grinned and tightened the embrace, cocooning her once more.

Millie settled gratefully against him.

"So Freya is the Countess of Henleigh?" Gabriel clarified.

She smiled. When Freya introduced her to the six members of the Kidnap Club it had been daunting. They used her shop as a hideout for the women they helped occasionally but her involvement was minimal. Her friend Lucy also aided them using her skills as a seamstress to create disguises, however, the three couples were the ones who took the real risks.

"Freya is a reporter. She met the earl—Guy—when investigating some strange disappearances. Little did she know, those disappearing women were women he was aiding."

"Because they needed to escape for some reason or other."

"Indeed."

"So these six people...they take the women in a false kidnapping and hide them somewhere...?"

"Marcus Russell, the earl's half-brother, kidnaps them, whilst Nash—

hides them somewhere until it's safe to leave the country. Guy makes most of the arrangements. Their wives all help." Millie chuckled. "Even Rosamunde helps with the kidnapping at times." She looked at Gabriel's stern profile. "I think you'd like her."

"She sounds as troublesome as you."

"Maybe not then," she murmured.

"I like you."

"You do?"

He smirked. "When you are not injuring yourself or sticking hatpins in me."

She grimaced. "I was fighting for my life if you recall."

"You certainly did that."

"So Rosamunde aids her husband, Marcus,

with kidnapping?" Gabriel shook his head. "It's no wonder no one has ever discovered them. Who would expect earls and viscounts and daughters of lords to be involved in such schemes?"

"That's why it works so perfectly. No one would ever think to question them." She held up a hand, her fingers splayed, and lifted one finger on her other hand. "The final official member is Grace. She was actually kidnapped once in a bid to hide from an arranged marriage and Nash fell in love with her." Her lips curved. "It's rather romantic actually."

A dark brow lifted. "I have now performed a kidnapping and I did not find you insulting me and trying to run away romantic at all."

She pressed her lips together. Admittedly, not much of the experience had been romantic but the kiss by the fire...there was no denying she would never forget that. Even if she should. After all, the man had killed someone. And taken her against her will. Lord or not, she should be wary around him, no matter how much she found her heart stretching out to help the scarred man.

"I'll send word to Freya when we return," she said firmly. "The Kidnap Club can help you." And she would likely never see Gabriel again. Which would be good.

Would it not?

***

The shop front offered little to spark one's interest, save from a modest sign hanging from a wrought iron pole. 'Strong Fabrics' had been care-fully painted on in a hand Gabriel imagined was Miss Strong's own. The windows were grimy and inside, the only things of note were a few crates and baskets, stacked haphazardly.

He wouldn't reveal he had already come past the shop when he found about her. The location—close to Trafalgar—had led him to the assumption she was funded by her father but seeing her beam-ing pride as they approached the bevel-windowed building, he knew she had not been lying about her having achieved this alone. Given the four days they had spent together, it no longer surprised him that a woman of so few means could achieve such a feat. Despite his privileged birth, he wasn't an idiot when it came to the value of things. Letting this shop would have cost her a sizable sum.

He'd released her from his embrace some time before they entered the busy London streets and he felt oddly empty not having her tucked up against him. He shook his head as he clambered down from the driver's seat, then walked around to hand her down. Too late, of course. She was already on the pavement.

Before he followed her to the shop door, he heard a bellow, and spotted a blur of movement be-fore pain burst through his face. Gabriel instinct-ively clutched his face and swung wide but he found his hand caught in the grip of a man easily as large as he and almost as scar-riddled—though he had both eyes, he thought enviously for the briefest second before another man snatched his free hand, preventing him from mounting a defense. Both men shoved him up against the wall of the shop and he heard Miss Strong's scream.

He'd given up fighting long ago—he'd seen enough blood in his lifetime—but nothing made him want to swing his fists and break noses with his head more than her scream. Whoever these bastards were, he wasn't going to let them get to her.

"What did you do to her?" the second man asked.

Frowning, Gabriel eyed the well-dressed man. He recognized him but could not place him. Behind the pair who had him pinned was another man, dressed with even more refinement, his arms folded, tapping a booted foot on the pavement. Gabriel vaguely recognized him too, but what the devil did they want with him?

"Stop!" Miss Strong cried, and she gripped the arm of the biggest man.

"Get out of here," Gabriel shouted. "Run for Godsakes."

"It isn't what you think, Russell," she said as she tugged on the man's arm.

"Release me," Gabriel said through a clenched jaw, summoning all his strength to ready himself to tear away and take Miss Strong with him. But wait a moment? He looked to Miss Strong. "Russell?"

"I'll kill you," the man named Russell said as

though he had just suggested he'd like to take tea with him.

Gabriel eyed the small scars. Some could be attributed to war—shrapnel—or the slice of a bayonet, but not all. Whoever this man was, he'd lived quite the life. The other two, however, were free from scars and pockmarks, and wore clothing easily as valuable as his own.

"Who the devil are you?" Gabriel demanded.

"Did he harm you?" the second man asked. "Freya has been worried sick."

"He did not harm me," Miss Strong said. "And you must release him. I am absolutely fine and in no danger." She gripped Russell's arm. His grasp remained strong but the other man's hold relented, allowing Gabriel to tear his arm free.

He met Russell's gaze and saw the man's jaw tick. They stared at one another for several moments before Russell lifted a finger. "Move and I'll kill you."

Miss Strong rolled her eyes. "He will not."

"I will," he repeated. "With pleasure."

Gabriel remained where he was against the wall. Miss Strong might not think the man capable of killing in the streets of London, but he recognized a fellow soldier—a man willing to do whatever he must to survive.

"When you did not open the shop, Lucy came to Freya," the second man explained.

"And Guy gathered us all," added the third

man. "We've been looking for you."

"Well, you found me," Miss Strong said lightly. "And I am perfectly well."

"Someone saw you taken from the streets." Russell folded his arms and narrowed his stare at Gabriel. "In a carriage just like that." He jerked his head toward the plain closed carriage Gabriel had used to convey Miss Strong to the gamekeeper's cottage on his land.

"It was a bit of a misunderstanding," she explained. "And I am so sorry to worry your wife."

Gabriel scowled and skipped his gaze amongst the gathering of men, still debating his next move.

"I do not blame you, Millie," the man Gabriel assumed was Guy said. "I blame this bastard here. Mistake or not, who goes snatching women in the middle of the night?"

"Well..." Miss Strong gestured to the three of them. "Um..."

"That's different," said the un-named man. "It is...consensual..."

Letting his frown deepen, Gabriel rubbed his sore nose. Was this the Kidnap Club to which she had referred?

"I will explain everything, I promise." She motioned with both hands. "When might I see Freya? I think we need your help. All of you."

Russell fixed Gabriel with a stare. "You want help?"

"Want? No."

"We need your help," Miss Strong insisted.

Russell gave a begrudging nod, some sort of understanding passing between them. He stepped back and shrugged. "I have nothing better to do. Rosamunde has been preparing for the festive season and has already been complaining how awfully fed up she is."

The third man shrugged. "Grace will welcome the chance to do something useful while in confinement."

Guy looked to Miss Strong. "You trust this man?"

She cocked her head and eyed Gabriel. "Strangely enough, I do."

"Very well." Guy offered out his hand. "The Kidnap Club, at your service."

He didn't want the help, didn't even want to take the man's hand. Yet the confidence of these three men left him with no doubt they could do a hell of a lot better job than he had so far at trying to free his sister from the grasps of Westwick.

He shook Guy's hand. Painfully.

CHAPTER NINE

When Lucy enveloped her into her hold, Millie grimaced. She didn't think her absence would be so noted. She should have gone to see Lucy first rather than the shop.

"Does my mother know I was gone?" Millie asked.

Lucy shook her head. "I visited her yesterday to see if she knew anything, but it seems she did not and I did not want to worry her."

"Thank you," Millie said, squeezing her friend's hands. She smiled at Freya over her friend's shoulder, an attractive fair-haired woman dressed in a regal emerald gown that would have been made for her by Lucy. Despite now being a countess, Freya had come from circumstances only marginally better than she and Lucy and shared the same determination to rise above her circumstances. Though she doubted Freya had ever expected she might also marry above her circumstances.

"I am so sorry to worry you."

Freya shook her head. "It seems Lord Thornbury was the one to worry us."

"Well, yes, I suppose," she admitted.

"Shall we take tea and discuss the matter?" Freya gestured to the table by windows overlooking the streets.

Rosamunde, a stunning dark-haired woman with a bold smile, and a confident air about her, snatched a biscuit but remained standing. "I should rather hear about your experience. Russell says you gave Lord Thornbury quite the fight." Her eyes gleamed with interest.

Though Millie knew Rosamunde through her shop and Lucy's friendship with the Kidnap Club, they were only barely acquaintances. However, there was something about her open manner that made her want to spill every detail.

"I did what I had to," she said instead. They could not be distracted from the urgency of the matter. The banns are being read for Gabriel's sister this Sunday. It gave them three weeks to act. Or until Christmas Eve. She softened the statement with a smile. "But I shall tell all one day. Suffice to say, I did not make it easy on him."

"Excellent," Rosamunde said as she took a bite of biscuit.

Lucy sat first and Millie followed suit. She tried her best not to stare at the luxurious surroundings and the beautiful bone china but she could count on one finger the number of times she'd set foot in such a house. How Freya had gone from living so simply to such a life, she did not know. Lucy gave her a knowing smile. If it were not for being Freya's closest friend, a mere seamstress with a Jamaican mother and sailor father; she could never conceive of joining women of rank at tea.

Finally, Rosamunde sat and Freya followed.

"Are we to kidnap Emma?" Rosamunde asked. She pursed her lips. "I never did like the Duke of Westwick. He made some exceedingly rude comments to me before I met Russell. Thankfully, not a single man dare come near me these days. It is much more pleasant to attend balls now."

Millie wasn't surprised. Russell had a similar dark and dangerous air to Gabriel. If it were not for Westwick's rank, she would simply command them both to go threaten him and she was certain the man would wet his breeches and turn tail.

"We are not to kidnap her unless we must. Gabriel is her only family and, well, she has a child in the country. She does not wish to leave her."

Freya nodded. "Of course. It is not easy to leave one's family."

"We could just take her away before the wedding and bring her back after," Rosamunde suggested. "We have done similar before."

Millie shook her head. Her involvement with the Kidnap Club had been minimal—offering a hiding place at her shop occasionally or finding out information from customers. But she knew well enough their usual ploy would not work here. "If Gabriel is correct about Westwick, he will do whatever he must to have Emma. He's a rich, powerful man and could track her down easily enough, not to mention try to take her daughter from her. Lydia *is* his daughter after all."

Rosamunde made a face. "He has been married twice before. Both young wives, both similar in appearance to Emma."

A chill ran down her spine. "What happened to them?"

"One died after falling from a horse but the other...well, the circumstances behind her death were rather strange. She died of a sudden illness, but I saw her only days before and she appeared quite well." Rosamunde gave a shudder and took another biscuit, shoving it into her mouth in one go.

No wonder Gabriel wanted her free from this man's clutches. Not only had he forced himself upon Emma and put her through the most awful experience that had likely never left her, but there was also a chance he could have killed his second wife. If he really was her father, she was grateful she had never known him.

"My hope is we can find some information that we can use against him and ensure he releases Emma from the engagement," Millie explained.

"It would have to be something outrageous for

it to even affect a duke," Lucy pointed out.

"I can certainly look into the circumstances behind his second wife's death," Freya suggested.

"Any information we have, we should give to Grace," said Rosamunde. "She will be glad to be kept busy and no one has a mind as quick as hers."

Millie had yet to meet Grace, however, her intelligence was renowned amongst her friends and if these women trusted her, then she did too.

She pressed a finger to her mouth. "Gabriel shall have a hard time allowing us all to aid him, I should think."

"These men never know what is good for them," Rosamunde declared. "But I am certain you can persuade him. After all, there are seven of us—eight including you, Millie—and we can do far more than one man can do."

"And let us not forget his first instinct was to kidnap you," Freya said with a grin. "He cannot be the cleverest of men, so he needs our aid."

"I am not certain about that." She tried not to sigh when she thought of Gabriel. She had not seen him since yesterday and it left her feeling oddly empty. "He is a desperate man, that is all."

Freya chuckled. "Yes, and we know well desperate men do not always act in the cleverest of manners."

Millie nodded vaguely. She had to remember that. After all, his desperation might explain why he had kissed her, so she would be better off forgetting it ever happened.

***

When Gabriel caught sight of his sister's face peeking through the parlor room window, his heart dropped to his boots. The men of this supposed Kidnap Club were the determined sort, but he had this itching feeling deep in his gut that even the leader —the Earl of Henleigh—wasn't certain how they were to bring one of the most powerful men in the country down. The last thing Gabriel wanted to do was send his sister into hiding. Scandal be damned, he just could not bear the thought of her in some strange country, all alone. It had been the two of them since his brother died. How could he abandon her so? How could he risk young Lydia's life in some strange country? Even if they were to send them both away, it could not be the continent—the duke would find them with ease.

Before he'd even tugged off his gloves and shook away the specks of snow from his scarf, she was upon him, her eyes wide, hands twining about one another.

"Well?" she asked once the butler had left them.

He shook his head.

The loss of light in her eyes made his heart pull. With nine years between them, the contrast between them was defined in several ways—not just age. Whilst he was all scars, she was radiant beauty. At three-and-twenty, she had grown into a curvaceous woman and as much as he did not wish to think on the matter, he knew she attracted attention from the opposite sex.

Most especially the Duke of Westwick. The bastard had been interested in her for far too long.

He should just kill him.

"What happened?" Emma asked him, following him through to his study.

He had no intention of explaining the farce that had been Miss Strong's kidnapping. Far better that Emma remain in ignorance as to the levels he had sunk.

"Let's just say the duke did not think the leverage enough."

"Bastard," Emma muttered.

He'd scold her for her utterly unladylike language, but he felt a similar need to blurt such a sentiment.

"The banns are being read on Sunday," she reminded him.

"I know."

He tugged out a sheaf of paper, grabbed a quill and penned a swift letter without bothering to sit. Then he gathered up the stacks of letters he had from the duke himself and the investigators. He didn't have much hope that the earl and his group of men could find anything useful in the contents— God knew he had studied the information enough —but he would not begrudge a second or third set of eyes.

"Pass me the string." He took it from his sister, sliced it with his penknife and added his letter to the top before binding them all together.

"What are you doing?"

"We have help."

"We do?" His sister blinked several times. "You do?"

He gave a wry smile. He was not famed for accepting help from others. After returning from the war with his injuries Emma had tried to tend to him whilst he found his way around the world with one eye and a ghastly set of scars. He could admit now he had not been pleasant about declining her aid. No wonder his sister expressed surprise at the notion he would accept help in this matter.

"There is a group of men who are willing to help..." He rubbed his jaw. "It is hard to explain who they are—I have been sworn to secrecy."

"Even from me? Even though it is my fate we are speaking of?"

"Yes." Though who Emma would tell, he did not know. He had a suspicion any of her friends would not believe her if she told them of these three men, all wealthy, all powerful, went around kidnapping women. It was a hard concept for himself to swallow but if anyone had told him a few months ago he would be kidnapping women himself, he'd have suggested they head to Bedlam.

Of course, he hadn't kidnapped just anyone. He'd just so happened to take a woman with more courage than most of the officers he'd spent the war with, and with an unusual set of friends.

These men specialized in helping women in desperate circumstances. As much as he did not wish to accept aid, this situation was most certainly desperate. How could he consign his sister to a life with her attacker because of a mistake he made? Because he'd been rash and foolish and killed the wrong damned man? He should be paying for the blood spilled, not her.

"There is still hope," he assured her as he bound the bundle in paper and more string for good measure.

Lips pressed together, she eyed him.

"There is," he insisted. "We are not powerless and while there is breath in my body, you shall not marry him."

Emma's gaze narrowed. "You had better not dare do something foolish."

It was a little late for that. His kidnapping of Miss Strong had been exceedingly foolish.

Foolish and much more enjoyable than he'd anticipated. When she wasn't flinging long-winded insults at him or endangering herself, that was...

He lifted a shoulder. "I will do what I must to free you from the situation."

She sucked in a breath. "You will not call him out..."

"If I must."

"You cannot shoot as you used to." She pressed

a hand to his arm. "Your sight...Gabriel, you must promise me not to do such a thing. We both know Westwick will not honor the rules of engagement. He shall kill you to be sure."

He smirked. "Not if I kill him first, and I'm as good a shot as ever."

"Then you shall be hung, to be sure! Your title will not save you if you have killed a duke, we both know that."

He took her hands, feeling the coolness against his fingertips and wishing he could give her more assurance. "I will not let you wed him, just be certain of that."

She withdrew her hands from his and lifted her chin. "I have been thinking on the matter and I think I should just wed him."

"No."

"He travels a lot. I shall likely barely see him. We shall be wed in name only and once he has my dowry, he shall be content. Perhaps I can live a peaceful life at one of the country estates."

Gabriel doubted it. He'd seen how Westwick looked at her. It was beyond obsession and that would not change once they were wed. "Emma..."

"I should rather wed him than see you harmed, Gabriel. You are the only family I have left."

"As are you," he reminded her. "And I will not see you consigned to such a fate, I swear it." He pressed a finger over her nose. "Do not fear. We have help now."

"Tell me about it."

Heaving out a breath, he met his sister's determined gaze. He supposed he owed her some truth at the very least. "These men take women—women who need to escape—and ensure they can run or hide without consequences."

She frowned. "They take women?"

"It's an interesting concept to be certain."

And one he was still trying to comprehend. How did one even find a need for such a service? Or keep it so secret for so long?

"They hide them or help them escape the country. By falsifying a kidnap, they can ensure the women flee without suffering any consequences."

His sister's expression darkened. "Oh, from awful husbands, you mean."

"Yes." The mere fact the need for such a service existed made bile rise in his throat. How desperate these women had to be to resort to such an act.

"Like the duke."

"Yes."

"I'm not going anywhere, though," she reminded him. "I cannot leave Lydia. What if Westwick decides to claim her and take her from me?"

"I know." He pulled her into the crook of his arm and kissed the top of her head. "I know."

Whatever he did, with or without the help of these men, he had to do it quickly and ensure nothing in his sister's life changed. She'd endured enough at the hands of Westwick already—

he could not bear it if she was forced to flee too.

CHAPTER TEN

Though a good head smaller than her, the way Lucy looked at Millie made her feel small indeed. Or at least left her wishing she had the ability to vanish. Of course, she could not blame her friend for peering at her as though she had returned from some foreign land declaring she'd been captured by a pirate king and was going to be his wife.

The Kidnap Club might have agreed to help them, and some strange masculine understanding had passed between them all, but she suspected Lucy was not going to forgive Gabriel for making her fret so easily.

Millie ran her hand lovingly over the silk spread across the table—a beautiful peachy pink fabric that cost more than many people would see in their lifetimes. Swathes of the fabric were already pinned around the dressmaker's dummy and though one could not fathom how it might look at present, before long it would be turned into a beautiful concoction that would draw eyes and many compliments at Christmas.

"You are lucky your mother did not fret," Lucy said around a mouthful of pins as she jabbed one aggressively into the fabric.

Millie draped her arm over the back of the spindly chair and rested her chin upon her forearm, grateful Lucy worked on a dummy and not a real customer at present. She rather felt like a fledgling musician at the feet of a composer, watching them tinkle away at the grand piano, when observing Lucy work.

She'd spent many an hour in Lucy's shop, even helping out at busy times, but watching her create gowns for the richest of society never got tiring, especially when her friend used fabric procured by Millie.

"I know, and I am sorry." Millie made a face. "At least the busy hours I am keeping meant she did not notice my absence."

"I lied," she mumbled. Frowning, her friend removed the pins from her mouth and set them aside before standing back to eye the gown in the making. "You know I do not like lying. Especially to your mother," she added.

"I know."

"I do not blame you. I blame that beast of a man —how is it possible he is a lord and what the devil was he thinking snatching you?"

Biting back a sigh at the mention of Gabriel, Millie forced her expression to remain neutral. Why thinking about him made her face do anything other than be utterly placid, she did not know. After all, their acquaintance might well be over. Although she knew of the Kidnap Club's existence by way of her connection with Lucy, she was not a member and only aided when necessary. Now she was no longer being held for ransom, her use was over.

And she might never see him again.

"He's more of a barbarian," she murmured.

The furrows of Lucy's face increased. "The man snatched you from the streets, not long before Christmas, and by the sounds of it kept you in appalling conditions..."

"Only at first..."

"And yet you talk of him with strange tones."

"Well, he was quite nice in the end."

Lucy shook her head and puffed out her cheeks. "Millie, did something happen with this man?"

"No!"

Unless one counted a kiss of course.

"Millie?"

"No," she protested again. *Unless* one counted a kiss one could never forget. "I just want to help him. His sister is in a terrible situation and you and I both know her life will be miserable if she is forced to marry that man. Goodness knows we have seen enough young ladies pass through our doors in similar situations."

Lucy drew out the chair opposite Millie and sat, placing her elbows on the table, and resting her chin upon her hands. "Do you really believe you are the daughter of a duke?"

Millie shrugged. "It is a little hard to accept."

"Will you ask your mother?"

Wrinkling her nose, Millie eased out a breath. "How can I? She has always refused to speak of my father and it hurts her. What if he forced himself upon her too? What if I am the product of such a heinous act? I cannot bear to think upon it, let alone summon up such memories in my mother."

Lips pursed, Lucy nodded. "I understand, though I would want to know the truth personally."

"Perhaps the Kidnap Club will find out for certain in their investigations. Have you heard anything about what is happening?"

"Freya says the men are meeting tomorrow with your barbarian," Lucy said.

"He's not my—"

Lucy ignored her, tapping a finger to her mouth. "And they shall figure out who is doing what. Let us hope they come up with a better plan than simply taking an innocent woman captive." She touched the end of a pin. "Honestly, I should kill that man for what he did to you. Or at the very least, jab him a few times. Perhaps we can invite him in for a fitting..."

A little shiver travelled down Millie's spine,

landing low in her stomach. She'd been cold and hungry and had even injured herself. She should not blame Lucy for her anger. In fact, she should be feeling some too. After all, it had not been a pleasant experience.

At least not all of it. Being warm in his arms had not been too awful, or feeling how tenderly he touched her, or...

She shook her head. Why was it so hard to feel angry at Gabriel for his actions? Perhaps it was because Gabriel was doing whatever he must for his sister. Such traits struck something deep inside her. Scrabbling her way up from poverty had not been easy and though she was not out of it yet, she and her mother lived far more comfortably than ever before. Doing whatever was necessary had become a way of life and she kept that philosophy when dealing with others too. Foolish or not, she had sympathy for him and his sister.

"Well, I did put a hat pin in him," Millie said.

"Good!" Lucy slapped an open palm to the table. "No less than he deserves. I might not blame you for wanting to aid his sister, Millie, but he sounds like an awful sort of a man. I hope you do not soften to him."

Forcing a tight smile, Millie shook her head. "Of course not. He did kidnap me after all. Why should I soften toward him?"

***

The cottage outside of London offered a little

more comfort than the gamekeeper's dwelling but not much. With low beams, the smell of damp, and wind whistling through gaps in windows, it amused Gabriel to find the three men huddled inside the cold kitchen.

Before he knew what they were involved in, he never would have thought any of them willing to bear such discomforts. Despite his grizzled appearance, Marcus Russell was the half-brother of Guy, the Earl of Henleigh, and Nash was the heir to a viscountcy. Though Gabriel technically outranked two of them, he struggled to see himself as anything other than the brother who should never have inherited. Life as a military man had certainly not prepared him for the ways of the *ton.*

He didn't bother removing his coat and noted everyone remained in their outerwear. Not surprising considering the frost on the ground this morning and the steely, thick clouds that threatened snow. He smirked as he imagined them all snowed in, trapped in this decrepit building, and huddling even closer together for warmth. With any luck, the snow would stay away. He had too much to do to be caught with these three men.

All of whom still eyed him with distrust.

Russell and Lord Henleigh remained standing. Nash sat on a spindly chair, his boots upon the table and his arms folded. Gabriel did not much blame them for how they looked at him. They might have agreed to help, for Miss Strong's sake, but the circumstances behind their acquaintance were hardly pleasant.

Gabriel remained standing too and met each of their gazes firmly. He'd made a mistake in taking Miss Strong—he could admit that much—but he was not going to be cowed when Emma's fate was at stake.

"My wife has explained some of the situation but I would rather hear it from you."

Guy's jaw remained set. Gabriel had some work to do in gaining their trust, but he did not begrudge them that. From what Miss Strong told him, they were admirable men, pursuing admirable causes.

"And I want to know everything," Guy continued. "No lies, no half-truths. If we are to risk our necks for you, we must know everything."

"Not your neck," Russell muttered and for a moment Gabriel thought there was bad blood between the brothers until he saw the briefest, slanted grin from the large man.

"I understand," Gabriel said calmly.

"Even if we were risking our necks, Grace wouldn't be stopped. The blasted woman has been reading everything she can about Westwick." Nash rolled his eyes. "But at least she is no longer talking about coming out of confinement."

"You won't find much. I have had investigators looking into every part of his life." Gabriel ran a hand over his face, weary at the mere thought of how much information he'd dug up and discarded.

"He's sired Lord knows how many bastard children but he's shameless about the fact. He didn't even care when he thought Miss Strong was taken."

He forced himself to release his tightly clenched jaw. The woman deserved better. Did Westwick have any idea how beautiful she was? How strong and bold and clever she had grown up to be? Few ladies in her situation would rise so high above their circumstances. Several more years and she would be a wealthy merchant by his reckoning.

"So you took Millie in the hopes of forcing his hand?" Guy asked.

"Indeed."

"I would have taken him instead," Russell muttered.

"And you would have ended up in grave trouble," the earl pointed out.

"And Rosamunde would never have forgiven you." Nash chuckled. "You are all talk these days, Russell."

Russell ignored his friend. "We could still take him. Threaten him. Ensure he goes away scared enough to always look over his shoulder."

Gabriel shook his head. Lord knew, he'd considered just about every action, but the fact was, save from killing the man, there was no way to leave his sister untouched by it all. If he called him out and survived, he'd either have to flee or pay for what he did, leaving her alone. "My sister bore a child by him," he said bluntly. "That adds risk."

"Freya said as much," Guy stated.

"That information alone could ruin her." Gabriel eased out a breath, his chest tight. Lydia's birth had been a secret from society for four years. It went against his every instinct to share that information with anyone. Even those who looked after Lydia did not know of the nature of her conception or the lineage of her father.

"There is more," Gabriel continued.

Russell lifted a hand. "Perhaps it would be better if we remain in ignorance."

"Probably," Nash agreed.

Guy levelled his gaze between the two men, a silent communication passing between them before he finally nodded. "Very well. We will settle for most of the truth."

"You wanted the truth." He'd been silent for so long on matters, never sharing anything with anyone. Now he'd confided some of the sordid details of his life with Miss Strong, a part of him wanted to unburden it all. That woman had done something strange to him indeed.

Guy eyed him. "What do you want from us?"

"We can kidnap your sister," Nash suggested.

"I've thought of trying to hide her somewhere, but she refuses. She does not want to leave England or her child." His gut pulled at the idea of tearing his sister away from four-year-old Lydia, who knew full well who her mother was and lived comfortably in the far reaches of Somerset—away from prying eyes.

"I cannot be everywhere," he told the men. "Westwick is coming to London in preparation for the nuptials and I intended to follow him. They will be wed in St. Paul's just prior to Christmas." A bitter taste rose in the back of his throat as he pictured his sister forced down the aisle to marry the bastard.

"Won't he recognize you?" Russell asked.

He shook his head. "I learned a few things during the war, but I should rather put one of you on him."

Russell's brows lifted.

"Westwick has a bailiff he uses to conduct most of his business. The man has a secretive past and he's known to be dangerous. I wish to follow him, but I need you to stay with Westwick," Gabriel suggested to Russell.

"Consider it done."

"We'll have Grace and Nash looking into his business dealings and anything else of interest," Guy said, then he took a step forward and fixed Gabriel with a serious look. "But you might want to consider the actions you will have to take if we can find nothing to disgrace the duke."

Gabriel met his gaze. "I know." He would do whatever he must to protect his sister, even if it meant giving up his own life.

"We do not have much time. Just over three weeks." Guy addressed the other men. "Let us do what we can to ensure this wedding does not go ahead. And that Lord Thornbury here does not have to do something drastic again."

He ignored the trickle of hope carving through him now he had the help of these men. He'd already failed once. Preparations should be made for the worst.

CHAPTER ELEVEN

Either Millie had outgrown her stays, or this was the most foolish idea ever.

Considering she'd always been on the skinny side, she doubted it was her stays. A hand pressed to her ribs, she drew in a deep breath and watched for the gleaming carriage to roll up outside the house. It took an eternity for the man to emerge once the footman had opened the door, as though he knew she was waiting for him with a heart that beat so hard it might well burst out of her chest and flop to the ground. As soon as she'd heard he was in London, she knew she had to see him.

Hastening forward once the footman moved away, she swiftly took in the expensive cut of his jacket, the shine on his boots and the fashionable manner in which he dressed. There was no denying he came from vast amounts of wealth. Considering the palatial house that occupied a large portion of the corner of Piccadilly she shouldn't have been surprised.

She supposed it just made it all the more difficult to believe he was her father.

"Westwick," she called.

He turned, glanced her over briefly, then motioned to the driver and continued toward the house as though he had not heard her.

She tried to get his attention again, then rushed to plant herself firmly in front of the wrought iron gates.

A gray eyebrow lifted. She fought to find some similarities between them but saw none. His lips were thin, pulled into a line of annoyance. His jaw was sharp, despite his age, his nose patrician. Either the jacket was cut to enhance his figure, or he still partook in plenty of exercise. She could see why he'd left a trail of brokenhearted women behind him throughout his years. The chill in his piercing blue eyes, however, made her shiver. She supposed they shared the color, but she prayed her eyes never looked as icy as that.

"I suggest you move before I have my man remove you." He glanced over his shoulder at the man who'd climbed out of the carriage before him. If she'd thought Gabriel dark and brooding, this man looked like a demon brought to life. Neither of these men made her feel the slightest bit warm or any more comfortable in her decision to confront him.

Swallowing, she lifted her chin. "If he touches me, you would be guilty of having him put his hands on your daughter."

He smirked. "Daughter? You are mistaken. I have two sons." His lips curved. "I do not sire weak females."

"You sired me to a Miss Mary Strong, do you not recall?" The words came out shakily, as though they did not belong to her.

The faintest flicker crossed his expression before being replaced by a growing smile. "I have met many women in my life."

Millie caught sight of the demonic man stepping forward, but Westwick waved a hand at him. Apparently he thought her no threat at all. The chances were she was no more of an annoyance to this ridiculously wealthy man than a single snowflake falling upon his shoulder.

Well, she might not have his wealth and power, but she would not be dismissed so easily, nor would her mother.

"My name is Millicent. I was kidnapped recently. You refused to pay a ransom."

"And yet you are here, looking..." He cast his gaze up and down her making her want to shrink into her sturdy boots. "Well enough, I suppose."

She glanced at the house. "I see you could have easily afforded it."

"What was the point when you are alive and

well?"

"I could have been killed and that would have been on your conscience."

He grinned, revealing even teeth. "Consciences are for peasants and paupers, my dear. Now if you'll excuse me—"

"Will you still force Miss Emma into wedding you?" she demanded, following his footsteps to prevent him from stepping around her.

"Force?" He shook his head. "It seems that brother of hers has been telling tales. What a strange sort of a kidnapping that must have been." He chuckled to himself. "I always knew Thornbury was weak but now it seems he has a woman doing his work for him." He sighed and pointed a gloved finger at her. "You may not understand how these things work but Lady Emma shall be a *duchess*. She will be almost as powerful as the queen. There is no need to force anything. She shall be grateful for her elevation through the ranks."

"She does not want to marry you." She kept her voice firm but he must have caught her hesitation.

It wasn't that she did not believe Gabriel, it was just that...well, he had kidnapped her and now it seemed rather ridiculous to be believing her kidnapper over a duke. Maybe he really was not her father.

"Many, *many* women want me." Westwick's smile grew devious. "Including your mother once upon a time. I do hope she is well."

Millie sucked down a sharp breath as he moved away from her before she could gather herself. His man barged past, shoving his shoulder brutally into hers and closing the gate swiftly behind them both. She twisted to eye Westwick through the black bars as he turned back.

"Give her a shilling and tell her to make herself scarce," he told the man.

He nodded, strode over and thrust a coin between the bars. Cheeks hot, Millie stared at the coin. A shilling? That was all she was worth to him?

"I do not want his coin," she spat.

The man shrugged, his eyes dark beneath the large brim of his hat, his expression utterly blank. "You will not be getting anything more, and if I see you here again, your mother will have more to worry about than feeding her bastard child."

She opened her mouth and failed to summon a response to the threat while her pulse thundered through her, leaving her knees feeling weak. The duke was vile, as was his manservant. Gabriel had been right about everything.

***

Hands fisted at his side, Gabriel marched toward the shop. Crates remained stacked in front of the window, shielding his view of Miss Strong, but he knew she was in there. He'd seen her enter.

He'd also seen her confront her father, unable to resist watching for Westwick's arrival despite ordering Russell to follow him. Were it not for the fact he was meant to be remaining surreptitious, he would have prevented the entire interaction. He pushed open the creaky door and glanced at the rusty hinges. Those would need replacing.

He shook his head and peered into the shaded depths of the shop. Hinges didn't matter. What did matter was the blasted, brazen woman putting herself in danger.

Tucked amongst carefully folded piles of fabric, she either didn't hear him enter or was too preoccupied with tugging out lengths and lengths of ribbon from the crate in front of her. He swallowed the tightness in his throat. The walk from Piccadilly to her shop had pinkened her cheeks and her lips were pursed with concentration. He sighed. She'd make his life a lot easier if she'd cease being so attractive.

Her gaze shot up when he stood on a squeaky floorboard. That needed replacing too.

"Gabriel." A slight smile curved her lips before vanishing when she met his gaze.

He almost regretted his no doubt thunderous expression, wishing he could bring back the smile. Who knew when the last time anyone apart from his sister smiled at him? His first fiancée certainly had not when he returned with his war wounds.

"What is the matter?"

"What is the matter?" he repeated, unable to believe she could be so oblivious. "You spoke to your father."

"How did you know about that?"

"I saw the whole thing."

"You were watching?" Miss Strong frowned as the white lace ribbon she held became tangled about her fingers.

"How did you even know he was in London?"

She eyed him, a brow arched. "A duke coming to London will be written about, Gabriel."

"You shouldn't have gone near him." He closed the gap between them.

Her gaze ran briefly up and down him but instead of shrinking away as he'd hoped, she squared her shoulders. "You tell me my father is a duke, and a terrible man at that, and you expect me not to talk to him?"

"Yes, damn it."

"Then you really do not know me at all."

He ground his teeth together. Oh, he knew her. He wasn't even surprised when he saw her standing outside the duke's house. Naturally, she was going to involve herself.

"You should not have gone there," he said firmly.

"I thought I could help, you know." Scowling, she looped and unlooped the ribbon, creating even more of a mess.

Rather like she had caused more of a mess with her father. "The duke is a dangerous man. I thought I had made that clear."

"What was he going to do? Murder me in the

streets?" She sniffed. "Besides, I hardly think one of his bastard children appearing even caused him a single moment of concern."

Gabriel winced at the coarse language, despite his own hardly having been polite. He hated that she thought herself a bastard—an unwanted, illegitimate child. The duke was a fool not to want anything to do with this courageous woman.

"His manservant made it clear enough the duke thought me no more than a mere speck of dirt carried in from the streets," she said coolly.

As neutral as her tone remained, he saw the flicker of pain in her eyes. It had hurt enough to know his own father didn't care much about him, but he could not fathom how it must feel to have your existence entirely ignored.

"The man's name is Bishop," he muttered. "You should stay away from him too."

"Do not forget you involved me in this, Gabriel."

"And I am removing you from this, *Miss Strong*."

"You think it is that easy?"

"Indeed." He nodded. "Because if you go to your father again, I shall be forced to kidnap you once more for your own safety."

"Do you not understand? The duke wants nothing to do with me. I am in no danger."

"That man is more dangerous than you realize. I want you nowhere near him." He glanced around the empty shop. She was all alone here. Vulnerable. "In fact, I think you should leave here. Go somewhere else for Christmas."

"I need to open my shop." Her hands went to her hips, despite the tangle of white around one hand. "And we are not all as privileged as you that we have country houses we can scarper off to." Her gaze clashed with his. "If you are so scared, why do you not go to the country?"

"I am *not* scared." A half-truth perhaps. He didn't fear for himself. He'd lost any fear the moment he'd stepped onto the battlefield amongst the roar of the cannons. But he was scared for her, and for his sister. If the duke thought he could treat Emma as though she scarcely mattered, what would he do to Miss Strong? No one would care if a duke harmed a mere shopkeeper.

Except for him.

"Perhaps if the situation was so dangerous, you should have thought twice before kidnapping me!"

He eased a breath through his nostrils. "I did not expect you to go thrust yourself into the path of a duke."

"And I did not expect to get kidnapped but here we are." She gestured wildly, then scowled at the ribbons and attempted to untwine her fingers again.

"Miss Strong—"

"And stop calling me that! You cannot kidnap me and shout at me, then pretend to be all civility."

He hesitated. It was easier to think of her as a miss. If he called her Millicent or Millie...well, there was too much familiarity.

"Millie," she said, sounding out the syllables as though teaching a child to speak.

"Your name doesn't matter, for Christ sakes. What matters is you getting yourself further..." he glanced at the ribbons while she continued to fight them... "tangled in this situation and putting yourself in danger. I won't..." He snatched one end of the ribbon and drew her close. "Oh Lord, come here and let me do that."

She fought briefly, then offered up her hand with a sigh. He unwound the ribbon slowly, allowing himself time to draw in a lungful of air, scented faintly with the herby fragrance of the shop and a tinge of soap.

It was a mistake. Because as soon as he smelled the clean fragrance of her, he met her gaze, and recognized how close he'd pulled her. She looked at him from under her lashes and his gloved hands brushed her bare fingers, kid leather upon pink fingertips.

It happened in a rush—a blur of movement that left him uncertain who had moved first. Her hands latched about his neck, and he grabbed her waist, then flattened his mouth to hers, hard and hot. She gasped and moved into him, her body impossibly close.

A mistake to be certain, but one he was utterly

unable to stop himself from making.

CHAPTER TWELVE

H is hands were there, hot on her body, leaving her feeling singed. Millie gripped the back of Gabriel's neck, torn between concentrating on the feel of his mouth, demanding and hungry upon hers, and his palms burning their way through her clothes.

Clothes which at present, felt very much a hinderance. When his tongue swept hers, she gasped and gripped his collar, and he bunched the back of her gown in one hand, pulling the fabric tight about her waist. Together, they staggered back several spaces until she knocked into a table. She barely felt the bump, especially when he used the opportunity to drag one hand down her side and grip her thigh through her skirts. His other hand pulled her hard against him, and he renewed his assault on her mouth.

Her mind whirled, unable to latch onto one single thought. All she was capable of was feeling. His lips, his body, the heat tearing through her and pooling low in her body.

When she took her next breath, he paused for the briefest moment. "Millie." The word came out as a raspy plea before he kissed her again.

Whatever he wanted from her, she wanted to give it to him. She'd never met a man more determined, more loyal. He would do anything for his sister, and it didn't even matter that he'd kidnapped her—she admired him.

"Millie?"

That didn't sound like Gabriel. And her mouth was on his so how could he have...?

She tore away from him, unable to go far thanks to the table. He eyed her for a few moments then his eyes widened when they heard the voice again.

"Millie?"

"My mother," she hissed, ducking behind the crates that had thankfully blocked her mother's view of them.

She hastened to straighten her skirts and put a hand to her hair. Strands hung loose from their pins and there was no saving it, but her mother was not unused to her looking wild after a long day's work. Maybe she wouldn't notice. Plastering on a smile, she popped her head around the stack of crates. "Mama, whatever are you doing here?"

Her mother lifted a basket. "Did you forget what day it is?"

"Um…" Millie eyed the basket, covered in a pale cloth, and searched her mind.

Dates, days, and anything else other than the hot sensation still pulsing through her body were gone. Her lips were swollen and she longed to either curl up for a nap or fling herself against the solid strength of Gabriel again.

Most likely the latter.

"It's time to make the Christmas pudding!" her mother declared, tutting. "You have been working so hard, you cannot even remember the day."

"Yes." She cleared her throat and swung a glance at Gabriel. "Working hard."

The man couldn't stay hidden forever and she doubted her mother was going to leave easily. Apparently he concluded the same as he stepped behind and around her so her mother had a full view of him.

"Oh!" Mama pressed a hand to her chest. "I did not realize you had company."

"Gabriel is, um, helping me with these crates." She stupidly tapped the top of one as though her mother didn't know what a crate was. "Too heavy for me, you see."

"Indeed," Gabriel agreed.

Her mother's gaze narrowed and she glanced Gabriel up and down, then smiled lightly. "Well,

Gabriel can help us now."

"Actually, I have to go, ma'am..."

"Nonsense. You can spare a few moments to make a Christmas pudding." Her mother's tone brokered no argument and Millie recognized the futility in trying to persuade her otherwise.

Her mother had not raised her alone by being a soft woman. Despite Mama being a head smaller than Millie, ashen-haired, and on the slender side, she still found herself very much at her command at times.

Her mother turned before Gabriel could mount a response and started setting out glass jars and paper bags of ingredients. "I thought as you could not come home to make the pudding, we could do it here. I have everything we need and when it is done, I shall take it home to boil then let it sit in the pantry."

Gabriel swung a befuddled glance at her, and she shrugged. "Looks like we are making pudding," she whispered.

"I, uh, am afraid to admit I have never made pudding in my life."

"Well, of course you have not, young man," her mother said without turning to him. "Men never partake in making pudding, though they really should. All these bachelor men never eat a single decent meal because they cannot cook a simple meal."

"I can see where you get your bold tongue

from," he murmured.

Millie smothered a laugh and went to her mother's side. "I was going to come home tonight," she told her.

"Yes, and it would be too dark and my eyes are not what they were. We would have made the ugliest pudding in all Christendom and goodness knows, I cannot rely on you to make anything without burning it."

"Mama..."

"My daughter," she told Gabriel, "is a terrible cook. She does not get it from me."

Gabriel's lips quirked as he shared a look with Millie. "Is she really?"

"Oh yes. She has ruined several excellent pans in her lifetime and once managed to create so much smoke everyone in London turned up at our house with buckets of sand and water."

"It was not *everyone* in London," Millie protested.

"It was a large proportion of the population," her mother countered. She took Gabriel's hand and his eyes widened. "Now, you come here." She tugged the large man closer to the table. "You can chop the prunes."

Millie half-expected the man to tear away and dash out of the shop but he took the knife after removing his gloves and methodically, and with painstaking precision, cut entirely even pieces of prunes.

She looked away from those capable hands, unable to decide what made her feel more heated—remembering those hands upon her or seeing him cut those blasted prunes. Lord help her, it seemed both scenarios sent a trickle of desire through her. And worse than that, she felt that softening around her heart—the one that made it impossible for her to deny anyone anything. Whatever this man needed from her, she was probably going to give it to him, even if it meant offering up her heart.

***

"I can see where you get your—"

"Bold tongue from," Millie said as she shut the shop door behind her mother and her pudding. "I know, you said that."

Mrs. Strong gave them a wave through the window, the pudding safely stored in her basket ready for steaming. Gabriel had never even thought about the preparations that went on to ready the festive meals that would adorn the grand dining table at Arden Hall. Now he knew practically everything about plum pudding. Today had not gone as planned.

Not least because he'd kissed Millie.

"I was going to say your resilience actually," he said through a slanted smile when Millie blinked a few times.

"Oh."

He wished he could go back to thinking of her as Miss Strong. Or even 'the woman.' He'd deliberately not thought of her as a person so he could gain the courage to kidnap her. Now he'd tumbled all the way from woman to Millie—the endearment everyone close to her used it seemed.

He did not need to be using an endearment.

Nor should he have kissed her.

A great many mistakes had been made today and he suspected he was going to make more. She shoved her hands into the front pocket of her apron and rocked onto her heels.

"So..."

"Do you really need assistance with the crates?" he asked before she could mention the kiss. Just a distraction technique, of course. He had no desire to spend any longer than necessary in the cramped confines of the shop.

"No."

Gabriel hooked his hands under one and gave it an experimental lift, grunting with exertion, then he fixed her with a look.

Her shoulders slumped. "Fine, I do."

"How did you get them in here in the first place?"

"Guy, Russell, and Nash helped."

He pressed his teeth together. He admired the men, respected them even. But they were all handsome, rich, and possessed both eyes. He did not much like the idea of Millie surrounded by three such men.

"Those noblemen helped you?"

"Well do not sound so surprised. They are decent men but you know as much already."

"Decent men," he muttered.

She folded her arms and cocked her head. "What is the manner of your disapproval?"

"Well, were you on your own with them?"

"Actually, Freya and Lucy were here, but why does that matter?"

"You are a lone woman and they are rich, powerful men."

"Who are happily married and desperately in love with their wives." She lifted her hands in the air. "In case it had not passed your notice, *we* are alone, and you are a rich, powerful, and handsome man."

"I wouldn't say handsome." And he struggled to believe she meant it. He'd scared away not one but two fiancées—not even able to persuade them his wealth and rank was worth being wed to such a face.

"No? Well..." She huffed out a breath and shook her head. "That is not the point. You cannot keep coming here and telling me what to do. Not about my father, not about my shop."

"This is my first time here," he pointed out.

"Second."

"Last time Russell prevented me from even stepping in the door."

"I should have simply let him beat you to a pulp. It would make my life much easier."

"Then I would not be here to help you." He tugged off his jacket, slinging it over a chair, then shoved his cufflinks through the holes of his shirtsleeves before putting them in his waistcoat pocket.

She stared at him as though he had more than a missing eye as he rolled up his sleeves. "Whatever are you doing?"

"Helping."

"You cannot."

"If you can accept the help of a damned earl and his friends, you can accept mine."

"But it's not..." She unfolded her arms and dropped them to her sides. "Fine. I need to open all of these, and these—" she gestured to a stack of brightly colored fabrics "—need putting over there." She motioned to the pigeonhole shelving lining one wall.

"And this?" He picked up the tangled lace ribbon that she'd wound around her fingers before he'd kissed her.

She snatched it from him. "I'll find a home for it."

"Good." He did not need it around, reminding him of how it had felt to explore her mouth.

Hell, he'd done more than explore her mouth. He'd explored her body too. Not enough of it, though. He'd felt her rear, the slender arch of her back, the gentle weight of her thigh.

But he'd wanted more. Much, much more.

Gabriel still did really. Even the visit from her mother could not dampen his desires for her. It was not just those lips and her stubborn expressions, it was everything about her. When she fought him, he no longer felt like a half-blind outcast of a viscount. He felt more alive than he had done since he returned from the war to find his brother dead and the legacy of the family in his hands.

Before he could utter something foolish, he turned away and opened the crate to delve into the pile of fabrics. They worked almost in silence, Millie issuing orders on occasion or refolding his clumsy attempts, giving up only when the dim light of two lamps prevented them from doing much more.

Millie put her hands to her hips and eyed the shop and he could not miss the pride beaming from her face. Westwick was a fool to want nothing to do with this woman.

"What did your father say, when you confronted him?"

Her smile dropped and he regretted the question, but he could not forget the original reason he'd come here. "Oh, he thought me nothing more than a mild annoyance, as expected."

"He is a vile excuse for a man."

"Agreed."

"And my warning remains. Stay away from him."

"You know I hoped to plead for mercy for your sister." She pressed her lips together. "He simply laughed at me."

He opened his mouth and closed it. How could he be angry at her for fighting for his sister's freedom?

"Just be cautious," he muttered.

Now the duke knew of her existence and what she looked like, he could well have placed her in danger. Gabriel could not fathom why Westwick might have nefarious plans for her but something in his bones told him he'd have to keep a close watch on Millie. He'd brought her into this mess and he'd be damned if he let her get harmed because of his actions.

CHAPTER THIRTEEN

The old shop had been so busy Millie should have scarcely had time to think about Gabriel, Lord...something or other, all day. She would have asked him to repeat his title but she kept getting distracted.

Mostly by The Kiss.

The Kiss to end all kisses. She hadn't reached the age of six-and-twenty without a few kisses but none of those fumbling and sometimes sloppy, soft attempts had felt anything like that.

She was fairly certain she and Gabriel had done something world changing, as though it had shifted the ground beneath them. As much as they had both tried to ignore the kiss, she couldn't forget it.

Now, she was not even certain she could step

foot in the new shop, even though she desperately needed to finish putting away those fabrics Gabriel had unpacked for her. She put a hand to the back of her neck and massaged the tight knot there while smiling and bidding good day to the latest customer, a sheath of calico wrapped in paper under one arm.

She'd hoped to leave early but the steady stream of customers wouldn't allow her to abandon young Betsy, who struggled with noting the purchases, and whose speech was a little slow. Her assistant was a hard worker, though, and that more than made up for the sneering looks she'd get from less pleasant customers or the time it took to write in the ledger. Millie didn't want customers who were rude anyway. In her experience, they were never happy, and would only make her job more difficult.

She finished tying another parcel ready for collection and began work on cutting the lengths of diaphanous silver muslin that she would drop over to Lucy's on the way to the new shop. She had to go, no matter what memories of Gabriel were there now. Too much had been invested in opening before Christmas and all her customers were looking forward to the opening. One way or another, she would push that kiss aside and do what she had always done—work hard to achieve her goals.

No lord was going to prevent that.

"Millie?" Betsy, her red cheeks bringing out the

soft freckles dancing across her face, waved a hand in front of her face. "Millie?"

Blinking, Millie smiled swiftly. "Yes?"

"There's a lady asking to see you." Betsy jerked a thumb toward the doorway where a lovely, dark-haired young woman stood, her white gloved hands clutched around the handle of an umbrella.

"Can you assist her, Betsy? I must get this done for Mr. Humphries. He intends to collect today." She gestured to the length of fabric she was halfway through cutting.

"She asked for you."

With a nod, Millie set down the scissors and eased past two excitable young women looking at her selection of ribbons to greet the customer. Dark eyes matched her glossy dark hair, framed by lashes that made her eyes seem astonishingly wide against petite features.

"Are you Millicent Strong?" the woman asked, her voice deeper than anticipated but tinged with a slight tremor.

"I am." She offered a reassuring smile. "How can I help?"

She glanced around. "Might we speak in private?"

Frowning, Millie hesitated.

"It is about my brother—Lord Thornbury."

"Your brother?" She spilled the exclamation before she could prevent herself. Now she saw the resemblance—the same intense eyes, a feminine version of his nose—but any mention of Gabriel still made her heart jolt. "You are Lady Emma?"

The woman's lips curved softly. "I'd prefer Emma if you do not mind. And I hope I can call you Millie, considering our...connection."

"Of course." As another customer left, Millie offered them a pleasant goodbye, then gestured for Emma to follow her into the store room. She grimaced at the chaotic scene it presented with much of her supplies scattered across a table or spilling out of the wooden boxes she intended to take to the new shop. "Forgive the mess," she muttered.

"Gabriel says you are opening a new shop."

Millie turned to eye the woman, who seemed almost ghostly in the gloomy light of the store room, her pale muslin hugging a slim but curvaceous figure. No wonder Westwick was desperate to marry her. Few great beauties had anything on this young lady.

It made her feel hideously dirty and unkempt to be standing next to this woman. She had looked no better yesterday either. Whatever had prompted Gabriel to kiss her?

"Gabriel spoke of the shop?"

Emma nodded, biting briefly on her bottom lip. "He has told me all about you." She glanced at the floor. "I must say I am sorry about the circumstances under which you met my brother. I hope you understand that he is a good, good man, and this situation is just..."

Millie held up a palm. "I know, and I do understand." She wrinkled her nose. "Well, sort of. It was rather a desperate plan."

"We are desperate," Emma agreed.

"I know."

"Gabriel says you are helping us."

"I have not done much, I am afraid, but I have introduced him to some men who can help, and I will do anything else I can."

She nodded again and peered around the store room. Several beats of silence passed.

"Emma, what is it you need?" Millie finally asked.

"My brother trusts you," she blurted.

"Yes…" Did he? She wasn't so certain. After all, the last time she had seen him, he'd been scolding her for seeing her father.

And kissing her. And making pudding with her mother…

"I fear he will put himself in danger over this Westwick matter. I have tried to tell him that I would rather wed the man than see him harmed, but Gabriel can be…reckless."

"Oh yes, I know."

"I suppose you do." Emma gave a rueful smile. "He is lucky you forgave him for the kidnapping."

"Yes. The kidnapping," she said vaguely. Somehow, being snatched by Gabriel was a long distant memory, buried under recollections of hot touches and demanding kisses.

"Ever since he went to war, he has been a little...bolder. I think it has something to do with being so close to death," Emma mused. "Of course, he settled down as much as a lord must when my brother died and he became viscount."

"You had a brother?"

"Did Gabriel not tell you?"

Millie ignored the flush of heat in her cheeks. It pained her to realize how little she knew of Gabriel. If anyone asked her of him, she could describe how he smelled or how his chest felt under her palms, but she could not offer many more details, apart from the fact he was far more noble than even he seemed to realize.

"Harry died shortly before the war ended—just weeks before in fact. He'd always been of such good health so it shocked us both. Goodness knows, Gabriel never anticipated inheriting the title."

"I see."

"Gabriel was injured right at the end of the war too." She shook her head. "It was all so senseless—many men died in those last days and for what?"

"It is senseless," Millie agreed, hoping it might prompt Emma to tell her more.

Emma waved a hand. "Anyway, I really came here to ask you to look after my brother. He might seem intimidating but from what he told me, you are not one to be scared away by his grumpy ways."

Grumpy. Ha, that was one way to describe him. She imagined most people considered him more on the formidable side.

"He is the best of brothers and has been through a lot. I should rather be wed to that vile man than see him harmed," she continued.

"I should like to see him unharmed too," Millie agreed. "But we must find a way to ensure the wedding does not go ahead too. Your brother would never forgive himself if you were consigned to such a life."

Emma's expression brightened. "See? You know he is more than just a grump too."

"Well..."

"I had better dash. Gabriel said your shop is quite in demand and I know you are busy. But, please, can you ask these men to keep a close eye on him and ensure he does not do anything rash? Perhaps you can talk with him too. He respects your opinion—I can tell."

Really, she would be better off putting Gabriel from her mind and letting the Kidnap Club manage this situation. She would have to tell her no—that Gabriel wasn't going to listen to her anyway, no matter how much Emma thought he respected her.

"Of course I can," she heard herself saying instead.

***

Usually Gabriel would welcome a distraction from the mountain of correspondence piled upon the study desk. He'd always been an active man, preferring shooting, riding, and the odd fight as opposed to letter writing and academic pursuits. It was days like today he resented inheriting the title. Everyone knew Harry was far more suited to the role of viscount than he.

Besides, he should be out there, doing something useful to bring down Westwick. While he couldn't neglect his duties, and Bishop would have to wait, he was itching to be back on the streets of London.

He cracked his knuckles and looked to the butler who had just entered. As soon as Gabriel saw his expression, his skin almost grey with tension, the correspondence suddenly became all the more appealing.

"His Grace, the Duke of Westwick is here to see you, my lord."

Gabriel slammed a hand upon the desk. "Damn the man."

"Should I..." Peters gestured vaguely toward the door.

Gabriel made no secret of his dislike of Westwick though none of the servants knew the full and sordid details behind what the man had done to anger their master. Regardless, from the chatter he'd overheard, none of the servants liked him much either.

"I'll see him." Gabriel waved a hand and sighed. "Put him in the Queen Anne room. I want him far away from the front door, and if Emma returns during his visit, tell her he is here."

"Of course, my lord."

Gabriel took his time straightening the letters and ledgers, putting away the quill and fresh paper then donning his jacket. He glanced in the hallway mirror and regretted it. He'd been fairly handsome once upon a time. Now it was all angry scars and a giant mess where his eye was meant to be. Why Millie had responded to his kiss so, he did not know. He certainly didn't see anything kissable in his reflection and yet it had been the most passionate kiss of his life. Could she really have faked such passion? And why?

Shaking his head at himself, he straightened his shoulders, and headed toward the room tucked toward the rear of the house. Decorated for his father's taste with a hint of Scottish flair that seemed entirely unsuited to fashionable London, neither he nor his sister used it much, but if he was honest, he hardly used the other drawing rooms either. If it was not for these upcoming nuptials that better never happen, he would be nowhere near London. Watching people's reaction to him, no matter how carefully they tried to hide it, grew tiring.

Westwick remained seated by the crackling fire, scarcely acknowledging his entrance into the room with his face turned toward the flames. The glow lit up one side of his face, deepening the shadows in his face, making his already square jaw and sharp nose more savage. It took all Gabriel's willpower not to jump on him, knock the chair to the floor, and beat him senseless. If he wasn't all Emma and Lydia had, he wouldn't hesitate.

Moving around him, Gabriel placed himself in the duke's line of sight and remained standing, his hands clasped behind his back. "What do you want?" he demanded.

"Am I not allowed to visit with my fiancée?" His smile reminded Gabriel of what he imagined a snake might look like before it struck its prey.

"She's not here."

"Well, I can wait." He glanced at his fingernails, then buffed them on the lapel of his jacket. "I have time."

"I do not," Gabriel said forcefully. "I have business to which to attend."

"Ah yes, no doubt finding more little girls to send after me."

Pulse flaring instantly, Gabriel struggled to keep his expression neutral. "Leave Millie out of this."

"Millie?" Westwick's smile expanded. "How charming. You kidnap the girl, somehow persuade her to talk to me and now it seems you are using terms of endearment." He skimmed his gaze up and down Gabriel. "I would turn you in for kidnapping but who would care if a shopgirl went missing?"

He would, damn it. He pictured shoving him down. Driving his fist into his face again and again. Hearing the crunch of bone. Maybe adding a kick or two to the gut just to ensure the duke felt every ounce of his anger. Instead, he eased a breath through his nostrils.

"No doubt you would know much about women going missing," Gabriel replied. "Your second wife...where exactly did she go?"

Any hint of a smile vanished, and he narrowed his gaze. "She died. I grieved most heartily for her."

Gabriel laughed, spying nothing but coolness and calculation in the duke's gaze. "I do not think you are capable of such emotions."

Westwick rose abruptly. "You have no idea what I am capable of," he hissed and thrust a finger toward him. "But let me assure you—"

"Why Emma anyway? Surely there are a hundred women desperate to be on the arm of a duke? Why not find yourself some biddable woman? My sister shall never be the sort of wife you desire."

Westwick drew in an audible, shaky breath, and closed his eyes briefly. The strange, far-away look that entered his eyes made a shiver trail up Gabriel's spine. "I desire Emma above anyone else, and I *will* have her again."

His gaze flickered sideways and Gabriel's gut dropped. Either Emma had ignored Peters' instructions or hadn't seen the butler. Gabriel twisted to the side to spot his sister frozen in the doorway.

"And there she is." Westwick grinned and strode toward her. "A vision as always." He took her arm and Gabriel saw the fabric of her gown bunch under the firm grip. "I just wanted to remind you that our banns shall be read this Sunday. I am looking forward to hearing them with you at my side."

Emma managed a vague noise before Westwick kissed her gently on the cheek. He gave her arm a squeeze and Emma winced.

"Until Sunday then."

Before Gabriel could follow him out, Emma stepped in front of him. "Do not," she begged.

He glanced at his sister, then at the empty doorway and tried to swallow past the hot, rasping breaths in his throat.

"You won't marry him," he assured her. "Not while I still live and breathe."

And maybe not after that either. If he could make certain she was taken care of, he would do what he must—even if it meant standing trial for killing a duke.

CHAPTER FOURTEEN

Though Freya lingered in the shop and tried to look patient, Millie caught the tapping of her fingers upon her folded arms and the constant biting of her lips. She bid the last customer farewell and hastened over.

Dressed in a beautiful wool pelisse, Freya somehow managed to inhabit two worlds looking simultaneously practical with a simple dark blue hat, no jewelry or ruffles, yet elegantly turned out in expensive fabrics. Millie wondered how she would cope if she was lifted from her world into that of the nobility.

Not that she would be, of course. Whatever that last kiss had been about, viscounts did not marry shopgirls. Freya had a little more respectability by way of her genteel but poor parents, though there were many who would say the fact that she still wrote for a newspaper now she was married was hardly what one classed as respectable.

"What is it?" Millie asked.

"Grace wants to see us. She believes she's discovered something."

"Have you told Gabriel? I-I mean Lord Thornbury?"

"Not yet. None of the men know. You know how they are—they shall act before we have even established if the information is correct."

Millie pursed her lips. Freya wasn't wrong but Gabriel would not be happy if he found out they were keeping him in the dark. Still, it was better that they find out for certain what Grace knew before telling Gabriel. The man might well do something reckless and she could not bear it if he was harmed.

Besides, she promised Emma she would take care of him.

They rode in Freya's carriage to just outside of London, passing the marker to Hertfordshire. Millie had never ventured this far out of London—unless one counted being kidnapped of course—and she appreciated the sight of gently sloping hills scattered with stone walls, farmhouses, and clusters of pine trees. Though her connections with the Kidnap Club had brought elements of adventure into her life, her role had always been minor and she'd never visited with any of the ladies at their country homes before.

Gabriel had probably toured all of Europe before the war and seen many exotic sights. Another reason why she should not dwell on him. He might have kissed her as though he was a dying man and she was the cure but their differences could not be more pronounced. He'd seen the world. She'd only ever seen London.

The carriage came to a halt in front of a red brick house. Millie counted six windows on the bottom and seven on top, all framed in white. This was no small country house, and when she stepped inside her suspicions were confirmed. Despite some of the decor appearing a little eccentric, with odd paintings of strange blurry figures and ornaments of cats as far as the eye could see, many of the furnishings were worth more than she could earn in a lifetime.

They were led to Grace who was tucked under a blanket by the fire in a cozy chair that appeared too big for her. Millie realized the delicate-looking woman was actually too small for the chair and it was almost a normal size. Her rounded belly was pronounced under the blanket and a strange ball of black and white uncurled itself, revealing the ugliest cat she had ever seen.

"Claude," Grace scolded. "You are prodding me." She grimaced, lifted the cat, and set it down upon the floor. "Forgive me if I do not rise. The baby has been kicking me all night and I'm exhausted."

Freya waved a hand. "If you move, I shall tell on you to Nash."

"You would not dare." Grace smiled. "I might be in a delicate condition but he is taking this protective husband lark a little far. I am lucky to be allowed to rise from my bed."

Freya motioned Millie forward. "Grace, this is Millie."

Millie dropped into a curtsey, then felt foolish when Grace waved a hand. "I have been reading about you." She fixed her with a piercing look.

"About me?"

"Well, all of you." Motioning to the sofa positioned directly in front of the fire, Grace tugged a battered notebook out from the side of the chair and flicked it open.

Millie and Freya hastened over to sit and Millie eyed the notepad, every page seemingly full of scrawled notes.

"It looks as though Westwick has fathered at least nine illegitimate children." Grace grimaced. "Forgive me, is that insensitive?"

Millie shrugged. "I have always known I am illegitimate."

"There does not seem to be much of note, as Lord Thornbury discovered in his investigations. A few did not survive infancy and none made a success of themselves." She pushed wire-rimmed glasses down her nose. "Until you." She whipped a pencil out from behind her ear. "How did you come to run a shop?"

"Um...is that important to the investigation?"

"Not at all." Grace waited, pencil poised.

"Can we get to Westwick?" Freya said softly.

"Oh yes." Grace flicked over another page. "Sorry, I love to take notes. It's..." She waved a hand, "how I make sense of the world."

"What did you discover?" Freya prompted.

"Well, his first marriage and the subsequent death of his wife does not spark any suspicion. He might have even loved her. However, his second marriage is something of a mystery. It seems he likes a certain sort of woman and unfortunately Emma is similar in appearance and circumstances. Both of his wives were lifted up through the ranks upon their marriage. However, his second wife vanished for a time according to the gossip columns, then her death was announced. Nash is struggling to find her death certificate for my notes."

Millie sucked in a sharp breath. "You think he killed his wife?"

"I think it quite likely."

"Well, we just need to prove that then." She glanced between Freya and Grace who did not appear nearly as excited by this information as she.

Freya sighed. "It would be hard to prove..."

"There is more, though." Brow furrowed, Grace perused her notes for so long Millie started counting the seconds passing by with each tick of the clock on the mantel. Finally, she set down her notebook.

"Westwick made several gains in the stock market after the war." She ticked off the fact on her finger. "The man who never leaves his side according to Russell is most decidedly of a criminal disposition." She lifted another finger. "But this is what I found most interesting...Westwick had a twin brother."

"A twin brother?" Millie repeated.

Grace nodded eagerly. "It seems he died well over twenty years ago so it is no wonder we know nothing of it. He was the younger twin and a feckless fellow according to the gentleman with whom I have corresponded. He was an estate manager who worked for Westwick when his brother was alive. But this twin, Frederick, died shortly after Westwick inherited his title."

"Another mysterious death?" asked Freya.

"Indeed. It might be because it was so long ago and I am only following the word of one man and no one would keep records of scandal sheets from decades ago, but I can find no mentions of this brother aside from a birth certificate. In fact, it appears there is no death certificate for him either."

Millie put a hand to her mouth. Two mysterious deaths and one man.

One exceedingly dangerous man it seemed. Whatever they did, they needed to get Emma far away from him and ensure Gabriel did not do anything rash. If he was capable of killing his second wife and his brother, he certainly would not think about having Gabriel murdered.

***

Snow fell from the sky, tiny white flakes dancing against the dark night. Despite the bitter evening biting Gabriel's face, the pebble road remained slick and shining under the light seeping from the inn windows.

The warmth of alcohol pulsed through his veins as he tightened his scarf about his face. Several men spilled from the inn behind him, raucous laughter echoing into a night only marred by the occasional rattle of carriage wheels. His own carriage remained at home, tucked in the stables behind the townhouse. There was no sense in bringing such an expensive vehicle to this area of London especially since he came here to forget who he was.

Ducking his head, he made his way down the road and cut through a tightly winding alleyway. It would take him at least half an hour to walk home, time enough for the cold air to eat away the alcoholic fumes surrounding him. Most of the stench came from his fellow drinkers but enough came from him.

He had never been one to drink himself senseless but just occasionally, he longed for the warm muddle of alcohol slowing his mind and softening the tightness the scars on his body caused. Now wasn't really the time to be indulging, he could admit that. However, the ache in his gut and a need to hide how he really felt from Emma had forced him out into the freezing night in a bid to rid himself of it.

It hadn't really worked. Of course, it hadn't. Ale couldn't defeat the twin emotions of desire and fury. They warred inside him, begging for attention, and he should be ignoring both. If he followed his desire, he'd be asking for another rejection, and if he gave into his fury at Westwick, he could ruin everything. However he eventually dealt with the man, he needed to be cool and careful. It wouldn't be easy to get to the man—he knew that from several days of following him.

It wouldn't be easy to forget Millie either but he had to try.

The sound of footsteps behind him made him pause and turn, forgetting Millie for the briefest, blissful moment. He peered along the dark edges of the buildings for several moments but saw no signs of movement. Waiting just a moment more, he gave up and moved at a quicker pace to reach the sanctuary of the wide, well-lit road ahead.

Footsteps again. He twisted sharply, ignoring the wrenching tightness the movement caused in his scars and saw a shadow flutter into a doorway. "Show yourself," he commanded.

When no one appeared, he stepped forward, muscles tense. Before he reached the doorway, a man rushed him, slamming straight into his chest. He recovered swiftly, fists raised, but not quickly enough. Something slammed into the back of his head.

Pain burst through his skull, making his vision white for a moment.

Gabriel twisted, able to make out the gnarly features of a man he knew well.

Bishop. The duke's man.

He spied a second man in the periphery of his vision and raised his arm before the wooden club fell again and it jarred against his arm, forcing a breath through his teeth. The other man, someone Gabriel wouldn't recognize even if he hadn't been struck over the head, punched him in the side, and Gabriel grunted.

Unable to block the next blow, Bishop struck his ribs once, twice. The next time Gabriel snatched the club from him and used it to wrench Bishop toward him and slam his skull straight into Bishop's. He felt a crack and heard a gasp of pain from the man but he paid for it—his vision swimming again.

Behind him, blows rained down and he twisted and moved like a madman trying to fend off a swarm of rats. Between the two men, they orchestrated a beating so vicious Gabriel was forced to his knees. Another blow to his ribs had him hunched over. He drew in painful breaths. All he had to do was survive. He'd done that before. Millie and his sister needed him. He knew well what this was—

Bishop didn't intend to kill him. This was a warning.

He swiped out and snatched the other man's wrist before the next hit, managing to draw him close and land a punch in his groin. He heard the gasped breath of pain and the man muttered several curse words before his hits ceased.

Bishop struck Gabriel once more over the back and then there was silence. Gabriel dropped fully to the ground, aware of the taste of blood in his mouth and scarcely able to see out of his good eye. The stone was cold beneath his cheek, almost comforting. He concentrated on drawing in deep, agonizing breaths and trying to figure out if Bishop was still there.

Voices from farther up the alley echoed between the buildings and he allowed his eye to close fully. With any luck, Bishop had fled and whoever they were would help.

And he'd see Millie again.

CHAPTER FIFTEEN

The sight of her warped reflection in the brass knocker made Millie wince. Even without the huge nose it gave her or the giant forehead, she was a sight. A morning of tending to customers, digging through stock, and chasing late payments had left her hair wild, her clothing creased and...was that a smudge of dirt upon her forehead? She gasped and leaned closer.

Oh Lord, it really was.

She fished a handkerchief out of the pocket of her cloak and rubbed her cheek furiously but the smudge did not appear to fade. What had she been thinking, turning up at Gabriel's grand house, standing at the front door as though she had every right to call upon a viscount?

Well, she had not been thinking really now

had she? As soon as word of the attack upon him reached her ears, she could think of nothing but getting to his side. Someone said he'd been stabbed, another customer claimed he'd been beaten senseless. Someone even said he was on his death bed, however Lady Lionel was prone to exaggeration.

He couldn't be on his deathbed, surely not?

She gave the smudge another furious rub and leaned closer to eye her image in the knocker. The door swung open abruptly and she leaped back.

An older gentleman with an impervious expression glanced her briefly up and down and released the faintest, "Yes?" as though she was scarcely worth him uttering the syllable.

"I, um, that is..." She lifted her chin. She might be the unwanted daughter of a duke but technically she had the blood of nobility running through her. "I am here to see Lord Thornbury," she announced with scarcely a tremor in her voice. There. That wasn't so bad, was it?

"His Lordship is not receiving visitors at present."

A breath she did not know she was holding escaped her. At least he was alive. The butler went to shut the door on her but before he could, Emma appeared in the gap and shoved open the door.

"Millie! What are you doing here?"

She held back a smirk at the butler's befuddled expression. "I heard your brother had been attacked. I wanted to make sure he was well."

"As well as can be." Emma's lips compressed. "He has bruised ribs at the very least but worse, his pride is horribly hurt." She swung a look at the stony-faced butler. "Oh let her in, Peters. She is hardly going to attack him, is she?"

The butler glanced her over, then took a step back, allowing Millie to enter. She deliberately kept her gaze upon Gabriel's sister and forced herself to remain expressionless as she moved into the entrance hall. Painted in muted tones, several vestibules held varying busts and a huge chandelier hung overhead. Two doors on either side led off to goodness knew where. More grandeur no doubt. She briefly glanced at her dirty boots upon the cream stone floor and forced herself not to look at the footprints she must have left behind.

"Forgive Mr. Peters. He is being overly protective since my brother was hurt."

"Is he badly injured? What happened?"

"He shall recover swiftly enough, knowing him, though he's quite the sight." Emma sighed. "He will not tell me much. The foolish man thinks he's protecting me."

"Might I see him?"

"A fine idea, actually." Emma's expression brightened. "Perhaps you can glean some information from him."

She led the way through one of the doors and up a wooden staircase. Millie followed, aware her heart beat so hard she felt her pulse in her fingertips. Was he in pain? Who had hurt him? And would they try again? What if next time they tried to do something worse—like kill him? The thought of never seeing him again made her stomach roll.

Emma eased open the door, gestured for Millie to wait, then met her in the hallway again. "He's awake and as grumpy as ever." She said this with a smile as she eased the door fully open for Millie to enter. "Let me know if you find anything out," she whispered before heading back downstairs.

Millie eyed the empty corridor and the open door. She supposed no one expected anything scandalous to happen between a shopkeeper and an injured viscount, and if it did, no one would really care. She didn't have a reputation to protect, after all. Regardless, she left the door open when she slipped into the bedroom.

Gabriel's gaze narrowed as soon as he spotted her. Or it narrowed marginally more. His one good eye was swollen and a gash marred the unscarred side of his face. He might have more injuries but the jagged scarring upon the other side of his face made it difficult to tell.

"What are you doing here?" he demanded, then eased up from the tangle of sheets about him, a sharp hiss escaping him while he attempted to shift his legs over the side of the bed.

Millie averted her gaze from bare legs underneath a long shirt and hastened forward to put a hand to his shoulder. "Don't you dare," she warned, dragging the sheet up over his legs. "For propriety's sake at the very least."

"You are in my bedchamber," he muttered. "Too late for propriety."

A flush of heat rolled through her. It was only a room. A room with a bed. A room with a bed with a viscount in it.

A half-dressed viscount.

A viscount she very much liked kissing.

Easing out a breath, she gave herself a mental shake. "I heard you were attacked. What happened?"

He swung a look at the open door. "The duke's man—Bishop. He caught me unawares."

"But why?"

"The duke is aware of our investigations into him."

She gasped. "Does he know of the Kidnap Club?"

"I doubt it." A groan escaped from his clenched teeth when he slid back into position upon his pillow. "The requests at parliament for information has probably drawn his attention but he no doubt thinks it's me. I do rather have a reputation for working alone." He offered a faint grin.

"That you do." She moved closer to the bed and adjusted the pillow. "Did he do a lot of damage?"

"I've suffered worse."

"That is not what I asked." She gave into temptation and touched his jaw, lifting it so she could view the damage done.

He met her gaze and she sensed the shift in him. His chest rose and fell as he drew in a deep breath, as she sketched her fingers carefully over the scars and new injuries, toward his lips.

"Millie..."

"Where else are you harmed?" she asked, and nudged his face this way and that, trying not to suck in a breath at the sight of bruises working their way down his neck. "Oh, Gabriel," she said, unable to keep the tears from welling in her eyes. "What did that rat-featured swine of a man do to you?"

***

Her fingers upon his face shouldn't have been comforting. They were rough at the ends from hard work yet Millie's touch was like a balm, reaching down to the deepest parts of him, slowly healing the wounds unseen. Gabriel couldn't fathom how she could touch him so tenderly when most people could not even bear to look upon him—but he took what she offered, closing his eyes when she skimmed her hand down his cheek, his neck, his collar bone. She tugged the open neck of his shirt and he snapped his eyes open.

"Millie," he warned on a growl.

"Your chest," she said softly. "It's bruised."

Bruised, battered, he couldn't care less. Not when her gaze met his and her pupils widened. There could not be a more inappropriate time for this but this woman summoned an uncomfortable response in him no matter what. He could be dying and he'd still want to kiss her.

He latched a hand around the back of her neck before she could move and brought her lips onto his. She made a sound of surprise and he released her instantly, cursing under his breath.

"Forgive me, I should not have—" He let his hand drop to his side, fisting it in the sheets.

She shook her head and sank onto the edge of the bed. "I wanted you to," she confessed, her gaze lowered.

"That noise. I thought..."

Her gaze lifted. "It surprised me. Your kisses always do."

"Always do." he repeated. "Yes, I have kissed you too many times, and for that I am sorry."

"What if I am not?"

His heart gave a jolt against his chest. "I find that hard to believe."

"Why? I am not some innocent debutante."

"So you think you do not deserve respect?"

Millie gave a soft smile. "That is not what I meant. I merely meant I am not frightened by a mere kiss."

Mere kiss? If any of their kisses were considered mere, he might as well give up and throw himself in the Thames. "I'm not a fool, Millie. I know women do not wish to kiss me. I am a viscount and I have to be aware of the privilege that brings. A woman like you might—"

She rose sharply from the bed, her expression bemused. "What? Fall into your arms because of your wealth and title?" She laughed. "Do not forget I fell into your arms when I thought you a barbarian."

"I *am* a barbarian."

"That is not true."

"I have the face of one." He smirked. "The temperament of one too. I have frightened many a woman off with both of them."

Cocking her head, she folded her arms and eyed him. "You think me scared by you?"

"No, of course not. I do not think you are scared of anything. But this face..." He gestured to his scars. "It is hardly the sort one wants to kiss on a regular basis."

Slowly, she eased onto the side of the bed again and he tried not to release a relieved breath. If she ran from him, it would bother him far more than any other woman leaving his side.

"It is a fine face."

"A fine face if one does not mind looking at a beast."

"How...how did you become injured?" she asked tentatively.

"The—"

She held up a hand. "The war, I know. But how?"

Gabriel should send her away but he owed her

something, surely? After kidnapping and kissing her, he couldn't bring himself to deny her questions, no matter how much he loathed talking of the day.

"It was near the end of the war at the Battle of Quatre-Bras. We were taken by surprise and my men were exhausted and low on morale."

She narrowed her gaze at him. "You went into battle with them, did you not? I would wager that as an officer you were not even meant to be there."

He lifted a shoulder and winced when pain speared through his side. "How could I send them to their deaths whilst I remained safe?"

"So you were injured at this battle?"

"I do not remember much. An explosion so loud it took me weeks to hear again, then darkness. I woke up back in England to find my brother had died mere weeks before and I was a practically crippled viscount with barely enough strength to stand, let alone manage an estate."

Her fingers lingered on his bare arm just below his shirt sleeve. "You are not crippled now and you do a fine job as a viscount."

"Know everything about being a viscount, do you?" he teased.

"In fact, I do." She lifted her chin and perfected a haughty look. "It involves ordering people around and pretending to be better than anyone."

He chuckled. "You are not far wrong."

"See? I'd make an excellent viscount."

Or viscountess.

He clamped down on that thought swiftly. Two women hadn't wanted such a job and Millie certainly would not. She might have the intelligence and determination for such a task but he couldn't confine her to such a situation where all she could expect was derision and the company of a half-blind husband.

Not that a few kisses meant marriage, of course. However, he would have to be cautious to avoid any future ones, lest either of them get the wrong idea.

Most of all him.

CHAPTER SIXTEEN

Millie smothered a giggle at the butler's stiff posture as he led her through the house and paused to announce her, with an inflection that implied he would rather be announcing he'd just stepped in horse droppings.

"Miss Millie Strong."

How someone inserted so much disdain in a mere name she did not know but she found it rather impressive. Whatever excuses Emma made for him, it was clear the butler did not think she belonged in Gabriel's house.

Honestly, she agreed with him, and in some respects was rather grateful for his snootiness. It reminded her of her place and she needed that reminder at present. She hadn't seen Gabriel in nearly ten days yet she had not ceased thinking of him.

Emma's expression brightened when Millie entered the drawing room. Surrounded by wreaths of brown paper, piles of varying garments, and what looked to be parcels of marzipan.

Emma appeared small from her position on the Persian rug. Millie's throat tightened when the woman rose. Emma *was* small, and young, and still due to wed the duke before Christmas. The women of the Kidnap Club had visited Millie at the new shop only days ago and their information on the duke offered nothing of use yet.

They were running out of time.

"Thank you, Peters," Emma said.

"Yes, thank you." Millie beamed at the butler, her amusement increasing when he gave a sniff and left the room.

Emma strode over to the bell pull. "Shall I ring for tea?"

"Oh no. I only came to deliver these ribbons." She lifted the parcel in her hands. "What are you using them for?"

"I'm making up the boxes for the servants and those that we'll deliver to on Christmas Day. Or at least my brother will." Emma bit down on her bottom lip. "I might not even be here."

"There's still time," Millie assured her in what she hoped was a brighter tone than she really felt.

Emma took a parcel and set it down upon a glossy side table, unwinding the string and drawing out a length of ribbon. "Oh these will finish the boxes so perfectly."

"Well, I shall—"

"Might you help?" Emma gestured at the mess upon the floor. "Then you can tell me about..." she lowered her voice, "you know what."

Millie pressed her lips together. The shop had been unusually quiet today. She suspected people were doing similar to Emma and readying for the festive period. "I suppose..."

"Wonderful."

Joining Emma on the floor after removing her coat and gloves, she tried not to think about her grimy boots upon the probably priceless rug and how rough she had to look against Emma's loveliness. Her muslin could not compare to the pale pink silk of the young woman's long-sleeved gown and she felt decidedly unornamented with not even a necklace in sight whereas jewels twinkled from Emma's ears and throat.

"Is there any news?" Emma asked as she flattened out a cut piece of paper and set some knitted gloves in it.

Millie winced at her eager tone. "Well..." She followed Emma's movements, stacking the presents, then wrapping them up before binding them in the pretty lace ribbon she'd brought with her. "There is something...that is...but it is not good news."

"You can tell me."

She swallowed. "The duke's second wife...it

looks like she may have taken her own life."

"Oh."

"Yes."

"So the duke was not involved?"

"No. She overdosed on laudanum."

Words hung unspoken between them. Why would a duchess go to such extremes as to kill herself? Millie had already jumped to the conclusion that her life with the duke was so miserable she could not stand to live in this world anymore.

"Do not despair. We still have this issue of the twin."

Emma nodded, a tight smile. "Yes."

"And there is time. We shall figure something out."

"Figure what out?"

Millie shot to her feet at the sound of Gabriel's deep timbre. Her heart might well have fluttered out of her chest and rebounded about the room for all she knew, because it certainly did not feel like it was in her chest anymore. Cravatless but in more of a state of dress than last time she saw him, the tall length of him made it hard to breathe, especially when she glanced at his lips and remembered the taste of him or let her gaze skim down to recall her palms upon his firm chest.

"We were just talking of, um..."

"The duke," Emma finished for her.

"If there is news, I would have hoped you would bring it to me." He stepped fully into the room, an eyebrow lifted while he surveyed the mess. "Was there an explosion?"

Explosion. All she could think on was what he told her about how he'd sustained his injuries. His gaze met hers and she realized he must have been thinking the same. Did he regret confessing such a thing to her? She would never regret knowing him better. After all, knowing of his bravery did nothing to diminish the overwhelming feelings rising in her, and she felt nothing but gratitude that he shared such a painful moment with her.

"How are you feeling?" Millie blurted.

"Almost well enough to be hunting down Bishop," he said.

"You would not." Emma gasped.

Millie nodded. "That gargoyle-faced monster of a man is too dangerous."

Gabriel's lips quirked. "I need to follow him, and now my ribs are practically healed, I can do so. If the duke is partaking in anything that will help us, Bishop will be doing the work for him, I guarantee it." He pressed a hand to his ribs. "I will be meeting with Russell later today at White's. He's been doing his best to keep me abreast of the man's moves."

Emma scowled. "You should be resting."

"Yes, you should."

He glanced between them both. "Nagged by my sister and my...friend. Whatever is a man to do?"

"You can aid us with these at the very least.

They are for your servants after all." Emma waved a length of ribbon at him and smiled at Millie. "Perhaps then we can persuade him of the folly of his actions."

Millie glanced his determined stance over with a rueful smile. She could scarcely persuade herself as to the folly of her steadily growing feelings let alone tell a viscount what to do.

"Doubtful. But we can try."

***

Resisting his sister's demands had never been easy but when combined with Millie's pleas, how could he refuse? So he found himself tying ribbons —or at least getting tangled in ribbons. He scowled at the mess he'd created about his fingers while he sat at the table and caught Millie's amused expression. He should wave his hand at her and demand her help seeing as he rescued her from ribbons previously, but he swore Emma kept swinging odd looks between them.

"Oh! I forgot..." His sister leaped up from the floor and hastened to the door.

"Forgot what?" he asked, making her pause in the doorway.

"Um, something."

She avoided his narrowed gaze, flittering away swiftly. Millie shrugged and drew out a long length of string for another parcel. Moments of silence ticked by. He wondered if she realized how hard it was not to look at her. She had the sort of uncomplicated beauty that needed no advertisement. No jewels could improve the slender length of her neck as she leaned this way and that, then pressed a hand to her lower back. No complicated gowns were needed to highlight her small waist. No feathers for her hair.

She captured his attention regardless.

And she noticed.

"What is it?"

"I was just wondering how you had time to aid my sister in this?" he lied.

"Emma is rather persuasive. Besides, it has been a quiet day at the shop."

"Ah." He glanced at the door. "Did she say anything of Westwick? I think this all a distraction for her."

"Not much."

Brow furrowed, he eyed her. She was hiding something from him but he could not fathom what. Russell had not let up on watching Bishop's movements and Nash stated as soon as his wife knew something of use, he would know too, but with these blasted healing ribs, he was feeling about as useful as a quill without ink.

"I am glad you came actually."

Her face brightened.

"Because I wanted to be certain you are being cautious."

Her shoulders dropped. "Of course I am."

"If Bishop hears that I have not ceased pursuing information on Westwick, you could be in danger too."

"Me? What of you? The man could have killed you."

He snorted. "It would take more than a few punches to do such a thing."

Millie set down a finished parcel, adding it to the pile. "Maybe you should leave it all to the Kidnap Club. They have experience with such matters."

"I have experience of danger in case you have not forgotten."

"Yet the man still managed to leave you with a broken rib!"

He rose sharply. "Because he snuck up on me like a coward and I was outnumbered! I will not be taken by surprise again."

"Why do you have to be such a thick-skulled b-b—"

"Barbarian?"

"Yes!" She shot to her feet. "I would try to think of a better insult but it suits you most perfectly."

"Perhaps I am simply a barbarian at heart."

"Who is determined to see himself harmed. How will Emma cope if you end up dead? How will—" She paused, inhaled an audible breath. "You have people who care for you, who care what happens to you."

"If you think the danger so great, you shall listen to my warnings then."

"I did! I haven't walked alone through London

once and my mother is under strict orders to open the door to no one though you try explaining that to such a curious woman."

"Well...good." He gave a sharp nod. "I am glad to hear it."

"And you will not heed your own warnings?"

"I am a man of action, Millie. Waiting around to heal has practically driven me out of my wits."

"I see." Something flickered in her gaze akin to disappointment, though he could not fathom why. "I will not take unnecessary risks, though."

He put a tentative hand to her arm.

"Good." Her chin lifted and registered the familiar tightening of his chest when he looked at her. God, he wished they'd met under other circumstances.

Her lips parted. He swore he heard her intake of breath.

"What is happening here?" she asked, softly.

"I don't know," was all he managed to say.

A noise from the hallway caught her attention and he took a step back before he gave in and kissed her here and now. At least he wasn't the only one feeling this, he supposed, but they had more important things to think about.

Like rescuing his sister.

"Have you spoken with the Kidnap Club?" he asked. "Guy said the women were to meet up soon."

"Indeed but they have nothing of use. There is mention that..." Her throat bobbed.

"Mention of what, Millie?"

"The last wife may have taken her own life," she whispered.

The words hung between them. "Does Emma know this?"

She nodded.

He shook his head and shoved a hand through his hair. "How the devil am I going to fix this situation, Millie?" he asked. "She cannot go through with this wedding. She cannot end up like his last wife."

"Emma is stronger than she looks," she reminded him. "But it shall not come to that. We have time, and we have some of the cleverest minds in all of England aiding us." She pressed her lips together. "I'm going to ask my mother about Westwick."

"You said it would hurt her greatly."

"I know, but I must do what I can."

"And what if...if the circumstances were like that of Lydia's birth?"

"What if I were born by such a heinous act, you mean?" Her chin rose and Gabriel couldn't help but admire the strength in her stance. She shrugged. "I had the love of my mother just as Lydia does hers. I can withstand the truth."

"Thank you," he managed to murmur through a tight throat. "You really do owe me less than nothing. I was your kidnapper after all."

Her lips quirked. "What can I say? Even barbarians need help sometimes."

The sound of a throat clearing made him take a step back. He ignored his sister's oddly smug smile as he left the room with a dip of his head but not before stealing one last look at Millie and silently acknowledging the way she made his heart jolt. Unfortunately, he wasn't going to be able to do a damned thing about it until his sister was safe.

CHAPTER SEVENTEEN

"**I** knew you'd be busy with opening your new shop, Millicent, but I did not know I would scarcely see you all festive season." Millie's mother set the foliage down on the table and Millie studied the greenery festooning the mantelpiece and along the picture rail.

"The decorations look lovely, Mama." She set her hat down upon the table that had a perpetual wobble no matter what they put underneath, and added her gloves to the pile.

Though the house was modest, it was always warm, filled with blankets, and furnishings which had been stuffed and mended and restuffed countless times. Life was not as hard as it once was for them but what a strange contrast it was to come from the tall open ceilings of Gabriel's home to the low-beamed, cozy parlor room of her mother's house.

Her mother gestured to the teapot. "I was just about to take tea. Do you have time to join me?"

"I do."

She sat and waited for her mother to pour the tea, then took the cup, aware the cup clattered against the saucer when she took it. Gulping down a deep breath, she reminded herself why she needed to have this conversation. It wasn't for her, it was for Emma.

However, she could not deny curiosity burned deep inside her. Was she really, truly the daughter of a duke? The daughter of such an awful man? And what had happened between him and her mother?

"Is something the matter?" Mama asked after sitting and taking a slow sip. "You do not seem yourself."

"I have been here all of a minute, Mama, how can I not seem myself?"

Her mother fixed her with a look and a raised eyebrow. "I'm your mother. I know you better than yourself." Her eyes widened and a slight smile curved her lips. "Is it that gentleman who was at your shop? I shall admit his appearance startled me a little but those arms..." Her mother made a squeezing gesture with her free hand.

"Mama!"

She lifted a shoulder. "I am old, not blind."

"He really is a gentleman."

"Yes, he certainly seemed so."

"No, he's an actual gentleman. A viscount."

Her mother's lips parted, then she took a quick sip of tea before setting her cup down upon the lamp table beside her. "I did not even address him correctly." She grimaced. "You could have warned me, Millicent."

"Gabriel does not think much of the etiquette of high society. I promise he was not offended."

"Why was he even helping you? Is he friends with Lady Henleigh?"

"Well in a way."

"He seemed fond of you."

"Mama, he is a viscount, and I am…" She gestured up and down her simple gown. "Me."

"Love does not understand rank."

"Love?" Millie spluttered on her next gulp of tea and discarded the cup entirely. None of this was the sort of conversation one should be having whilst drinking, she concluded.

"It would be easy to love a man like that and, admittedly I am biased, but you are quite the loveable sort of person."

Millie frowned. She'd never considered herself loveable. Too commanding, too determined, too hardworking. Not loveable.

But now the word was spinning around her mind again and again. She knew how easy it could be to love Gabriel but for him to love her in return…?

Unfathomable.

She inhaled deeply. There was no time to discuss this anyway. "Mama, the reason I know Gabriel is because his sister is, well, engaged to the Duke of Westwick." She watched her mother's expression for some flicker of something but saw nothing other than raised eyebrows.

"The Duke of Westwick," she repeated. "You worked in his household."

Mama narrowed her gaze. "Now, why do you wish to talk of that?"

"Because I know that..." Millie swallowed the increasingly growing knot in her throat. Why hiding this from her mother felt like a betrayal she did not know. After all, her mother had hidden who her father was her whole life. "I know that he is my father."

Her mother's mouth tightened. She snatched up the cup of tea, drained it swiftly and set it down again. "I see."

"It is true then?"

She gave a tiny shrug.

"Why did you never tell me? Was he...was he awful to you?"

She shook her head. "At least not until I found out I was with child. I was summarily told to leave the house with not even a letter of recommendation. He refused to see me ever again."

"I'm sorry, Mama."

"What is there to be sorry about? I have the

best daughter a mother could ask for."

"Was he...that is...why did you...?" Millie gestured vaguely. She did not really want to think about her mother taking a lover, especially a man like that.

"He was charming and told me he loved me. I was young and believed him, of course. Why, he even sent me love letters."

"Love letters?" Millie repeated. That hardly sounded like the Westwick she knew now.

"I do believe I was not alone in receiving such letters unfortunately. I think I have some still..." Her mother pressed a finger to her lips, then rose and vanished into the rear room.

Millie twined her fingers together and tapped them against one another. She could scarcely believe her mother had kept the letters let alone had been practically in love with the duke.

Her mother returned and handed her the correspondence. Millie unfolded the crinkled paper slowly and read professions of love and elegant words that would no doubt tempt many a woman into bed. There was even talk of her pregnancy and a marriage. Her mother was no fool but even Millie could not believe the Duke of Westwick really intended to marry her mother.

"He does not have that neat of a hand for a duke," Millie commented, pointing to the smudges on the paper.

"He used to, look." She lifted the top letter away

to reveal others more neatly penned. "I assumed he wrote the last in a rush and with pain in his heart when he sent me away." Her mother chuckled. "How wrong I was."

"I'm sorry if this hurts you, Mama, but I must know about him. Not for me but for Gabriel's sister."

"I cannot tell you much, I am afraid, but after the death of his brother I was told to leave and his true nature was revealed to me. He would not claim you or grant me any kind of audience. Initially, I concluded it was because it was too shameful, but I soon realized he had no love for me and when I went to work for Sir Morecambe after you were born, it became clear he never had any good intentions towards me."

"It seems he never changed, Mama. In fact, I believe his behavior grew worse."

Her mother's complexion paled. "I imagine as he aged women did not flock to him so easily. Despite his ability to pen such words, I understand now he did not have a heart or the ability to love."

Millie nodded grimly. She knew that much already, but the thought of Emma being on the receiving end of his behavior only fired her desire to free her from his clutches.

**

Drawing in a sharp breath through his teeth, Gabriel eased onto the chair and glanced around the gentlemen's club. His ribs panged and the bruises were still scattered across his body. But the pain wasn't nearly as discomforting as sitting in Boodle's. The last time he'd been here had been before the war.

Before cannon shot had turned him into a monster.

The waiter tried his best to maintain a natural expression as he placed a whiskey in front of him, but Gabriel caught the quick, curious look.

He ignored it and gestured to Nash's cup of coffee. "Not drinking?"

"With the baby here any day, I daren't. I need my wits about me."

Guy shook his head. "One whiskey won't addle you, Nash. I've seen you drink enough to fill a whiskey barrel and still be lucid enough to sing the National Anthem."

"I was celebrating my engagement to Grace," Nash reminded his friend. "And I'm fairly certain I did not get a single word right."

Guy smirked. "I was not exactly sober either so I cannot recall." He turned to Gabriel. "How are you healing?"

"I'm well enough," Gabriel muttered. "Even if my pride took a dent."

"That Bishop is an underhanded character. Russell has been dividing his time between Westwick and Bishop and, Lord knows, Bishop has plenty of people in Westwick's pocket, though we've seen nothing useful yet."

Gabriel tapped his fingers upon the table. "Time is running out."

Nash nodded. "Agreed. So we need to move more quickly, decisively. We've been chasing our tails for too long."

"Has Grace found much more on Westwick?" Guy asked.

"She's up to her chin in correspondence." He waved a hand. "Easily done I suppose given her height, but you know what I mean. She must have written a hundred letters to old employees of his but given the current weather, the post is frightfully slow."

"I've been trying to hunt down this former lover of Westwick's," Gabriel explained. "Has she had any luck there?"

"That Miss Cross?" Nash said.

"Indeed." Gabriel flattened out one of pages from the investigator he'd hired and jabbed a finger. "I went to the old address only yesterday, but no one has heard of her. Obviously, I am covering previously trod ground here but she's the only one I could not find. According to the investigator, she worked in Westwick's household before he inherited the title and one of the old valets had quite a bit to say about her—thought Westwick to be in love with her."

Nash nodded. "But she's vanished."

"It seems so."

"Too many people vanish around Westwick,"

Guy murmured.

Gabriel suppressed a shudder. He didn't want to think what might happen to Emma if she displeased him.

"Grace has been looking into her," Nash said, "though whether she has managed to correspond with anyone or find anything on her, I cannot say."

"If you find anything out, let me know," Gabriel said. "I need to be doing something useful, and following Bishop and Westwick around has led to nothing."

Guy rubbed a hand over his face and took a long gulp of his drink. "Bishop is at least aware you are actively trying to dig into Westwick's past. I doubt the man will do anything rash after attacking you."

"I wasted too much time hoping he'd slip," Gabriel admitted. "He's never been caught after all these years of serving Westwick—I doubt he's going to reveal anything now."

"We could always set Russell on him. See how he likes a beating." Nash shrugged and looked to Guy who nudged his arm. "What?"

"We cannot draw attention to Russell and our involvement, you bloody idiot."

"All I am saying is Russell is good with his fists and excellent at making people talk. One look at him and most people confess to sins they scarcely recall themselves. And if we do not help Emma, then what's the damned point in doing this."

Gabriel shook his head. "You cannot risk revealing your involvement. I would not wish you to jeopardize the club. Besides, if this face doesn't scare Bishop, I doubt Russell's will."

"We have a little more time," Guy assured him. "And we have some information. Grace is still looking into this idea of Westwick having made gains in the stock market and we know his brother accrued enormous debts before his death."

"His brother?" Gabriel repeated. "What the devil did I miss while I was recuperating?"

The two men shared a look. "I thought Millie would have told you," Guy explained.

No. The damned woman had been suspicious the last time he'd seen her but of course he'd been too wrapped up in trying not to kiss her to question her properly.

"He had a brother?"

"A twin," Guy said. "Died in his sleep it seems, though we're not certain on that. It was a over twenty years ago, hence why we didn't know about it, but he's scarcely mentioned with the exception of his name recorded in some ledgers."

He'd wager Millie was trying to protect him in some unknown way. She'd been worried for him last time he'd seen her, demanding he not act rashly. Why she thought he might act foolishly after such news, he wasn't certain, but he wished like hell she had been open with him.

Of course, he was not exactly being open with

her. If he truly was, he'd have told her how he fell for her just a fragment more every time he saw her.

How he didn't know what he would do if he didn't see her again once this nightmare was over.

If this nightmare was over.

"Grace thinks they were trying to hide something scandalous about the brother," Nash said. "Maybe about his manner of death, maybe about something worse than vast quantities of debt." He lifted his shoulders. "Who is to say?"

"So we need to find out about this twin." Gabriel ticked off a finger. "And about this Miss Cross." He ticked off another finger.

Guy nodded.

"Grace is already focusing her attentions there," Nash said, "but we should continue to speak with any of the servants and staff. I believe the women are doing their best to speak with those still residing in London."

"It might be worth gathering us all again soon so we can bring together all the information we have so far. Perhaps there is something we've missed," Guy suggested.

Gabriel curled his fists. Much more talk and no action and he might go out of his wits. But he would do what he must for his sister, even put aside his increasing desire for Millie, and focus on getting his sister out of this situation before someone got hurt. Again.

CHAPTER EIGHTEEN

Having almost the entire Kidnap Club gathered in one room disconcerted Millie. The beautifully modern drawing room of the earl's townhouse offered gleaming marble, elegant, muted tones of green, and simple molded ceilings. The building had suffered a fire over a year ago but with how it looked now, one would never know.

Each of the couples stood together, with the exception of Nash, who was seated at the piano, looking a little lost without his wife. She glanced at Freya and the earl, then back at Gabriel, aware they stood similarly.

Except they were not a couple.

And seeing the similar posture should not convince her they would be. Or that they could be. Freya did not come from wealth that much was true and was very much a working woman, however, her family background was more genteel than Millie's.

Far more genteel. Freya wasn't the bastard daughter of a duke, after all.

Stupidly, she kept watching their interactions; the little tender touches between them, the way Lord Henleigh leaned down and murmured in her ear and how Freya offered small, knowing smiles. Millie never had time for even the thought of romance before, but her heart gave a jealous pang. How wonderful would it be to have the support of the man she loved?

She swallowed past the tight knot in her chest and batted away the thoughts. They were here for Emma, nothing more.

Lord Henleigh spoke first. "I'll be frank, Gabriel. There is no doubting Westwick has abused his power but finding evidence of it is nigh on impossible."

Gabriel nodded solemnly, and the resigned expression on his face made her heart shrink. If the others were not here, she'd be fighting hard not to press herself to his chest and offer all the comfort she could.

"His man Bishop takes all of the risk," Gabriel said. "We need to focus on him."

"But he has done nothing these past weeks," Nash pointed out. "He knows you are following the duke's activities, and for the man to have gone unnoticed in his activities for so long, he cannot be foolish enough to do them under our noses."

"I know." Gabriel rubbed a hand across his jaw. "I know."

The earl shared a look with Freya who took a slight step forward. "It might be time to consider getting Emma away from here."

"She will not go," Millie answered for Gabriel.

"You need to persuade her," Rosamunde added.

"Or we can bloody well take her," suggested Russell who received a light tap on his arm from his wife. "What?" He shrugged.

Rosamunde rolled her eyes. "What my husband is saying is that we need to persuade her. From our investigations, it does look as though the earl's second wife killed herself—though it was well hidden."

Lord Henleigh frowned. "Did you know this?" he asked his wife.

Rosamunde held up a hand. "We wanted to be certain and we did not want certain members of this group acting all brash and drawing attention to themselves. We already know our requests for information from parliament drew attention." She nodded toward Gabriel. "Unfortunately for Lord Thornbury here, the suspicion landed entirely upon him."

"Not unfortunately at all," Gabriel replied. "Far better it land upon me than any of you."

"Anyway," Freya interrupted, "what Emma

needs to understand is we are not giving up on her." She fixed her focus on Gabriel and Millie. "We simply need more time."

"So we send Emma away for a while, until we can find something else about the duke?" Millie asked.

"Indeed," Freya said. "Ensure the wedding does not go ahead whilst we find something that shall ensure he has no sway over Gabriel and his sister, then bring her home."

Millie looked to Gabriel whose jaw twitched. "It's an idea. Surely there is somewhere we can send her?"

"I have a cousin in Ireland," Lord Henleigh suggested. "No one shall find her there as my cousin's presence there is...let's just say, unknown."

Gabriel nodded slowly. "She'll be reluctant. She shall not want to bring scandal upon us, *and* we have little idea how long it will take." He lowered his voice and murmured to Millie. "And what of her daughter?"

"Under the duke's firm hand, I suspect she shall not be able to see Lydia anyway."

His lips pressed into a thin line.

"What of the scandal of a runaway bride? Shall her reputation stay intact?" asked Millie.

"She will not need fear for her reputation," Guy explained. "She shall be kidnapped, much as we have done before."

Nash nodded. "Hardly her fault."

"Well," Freya asked. "Do you think you can persuade her?"

Gabriel looked to Millie who gave a slight nod. As far as she could see, it was their only option. Somehow, they would ensure the duke could never touch either of them again but as yet, they had no way of doing so. A few more weeks, maybe a month or so, and they could find something, surely? A man with a soul as black as her father's had to have erred somewhere.

"Will you help me talk to her?" Gabriel asked.

She smiled softly. As though she could deny him anything at this point.

***

Before they entered the music room, Millie took Gabriel's hand and squeezed his fingers between hers. They were still cool from the frosty day having seeped through her too thin gloves. He'd have to buy her some nice warm leather ones for Christmas, he concluded.

That was, if they continued to be in each other's lives. He'd been pushed away by two fiancées—neither of whom he particularly felt much for. Was admitting his feelings for Millie worth the risk?

She loosened her hand from his and he glanced at her.

Yes. Yes, she was.

After his sister was safe, he'd broach the subject. And try to figure out where the devil they went from here. That was if she wanted him, of course.

The scattered tinkle of the piano stopped when he opened the door and Emma rose immediately from the piano stool. "Any news? I do wish you had let me come. You should have persuaded him, Millie."

"The farther away from this situation you are the better. We cannot have Westwick getting suspicious about the Kidnap Club," Millie reminded her.

His sister puffed out her cheeks. "It's still so darned frustrating, sitting around, waiting for a verdict on one's fate."

He forewent scolding her for her language. He could think of far worse words than darned to describe the situation. The last thing he wanted was to send his sister away, out from under his protection for who knew how long.

"Well?" Emma pressed.

He grimaced and shared a look with Millie. She stepped forward but he put a hand out. Millie had done so much already—he wasn't going to force her to tell his sister of her fate. "We need more time."

Emma's eyes widened. "There is no time. The wedding is in a week!" She slumped onto the piano stool and propped her elbows on the keys, creating an ugly sound as she put her head in her hands. "I'm going to have to marry the man, am I not?"

Gabriel set his jaw. "No."

She lifted her head. "But what can we do? He will reveal everything if I break the engagement and it is bad enough that he shall reveal about Lydia but what of you? You could stand trial."

"We need you gone," Gabriel stated.

"Gone?"

"We talked of this before, Emma. We send you away."

"No." Her jaw thrust out. "I cannot leave Lydia for good. You know he will use her as leverage if I vanish. He will take her from me and—" Her voice cracked.

"It will just be for a while," Millie assured her softly. "Just until we have the full measure of the man. Then once we have what we need, we can bring you back and you can be reunited."

Emma's dark eyes were wide as she skipped her gaze between them. "But where shall I even go? And what is to stop Westwick from exacting revenge when I am gone?"

He blew out a breath. "Lord Henleigh has a cousin in Ireland. She is hiding from her violent husband there. You shall be entirely safe."

"And what of Westwick?"

"You're going to be kidnapped," Millie explained.

"Kidnapped?"

"It is not so terrible as it sounds." Millie smiled softly. "The Kidnap Club will fake your kidnapping. You shall vanish for a while and return unharmed once we have what we need to ensure Westwick never touches you again."

Gabriel nodded. "They have done it before. Westwick will not look like a man abandoned at the altar but instead a man whose fiancée was taken from him and he will appear callous indeed if he reveals the information he has about either of us, even if he does suspect it to be a ruse."

Emma rose slowly, closed the piano lid, and paced past the fireplace to peer out of the window then folded her arms about herself and faced them both. "You are both certain about this?"

"The Kidnap Club are experienced in such matters," Millie insisted. "Hence their name."

"And I shall not rest until you are brought home safely," Gabriel vowed.

"When is this kidnapping to occur?"

"Two days hence." As he uttered the words, his gut turned to ice. Surely there had to be a better way? But between all of them, they had not managed to find a better solution and the only other one meant sacrificing himself. He'd do it gladly, however, leaving Emma alone in the world made his chest tighten.

Emma tightened her grip around herself, bunching her hands into the fabric of her dress until her knuckles whitened. Doubt threatened to tear him asunder. Perhaps there was a better way. Perhaps he should be calling Westwick out for a dual and ensuring the man paid for his misdeeds with his life. He had no doubt his aim would be true —years at war had ensured that—but to put Emma through a trial and his subsequent hanging...

And to lose Millie for good...

"I will do it," Emma said.

Millie closed the gap and took his sister's hands in hers. "We will ensure you can return home. None of us shall give up on you, I promise."

Emma gave a tight smile. "Will you come with me?" she asked Millie. "To the kidnapping that is. I cannot bear to be alone."

Millie glanced at Gabriel and he knew she was weighing up the time she had left to open the shop and whether her charitable heart could deny Emma.

"We could send someone else," he suggested. "I am certain Rosamunde or Freya would—"

"I will go," Millie promised. "I will not be able to accompany you all of the way but you will be in capable hands."

Emma lifted her hands. "Well, Brother, looks like I am to be kidnapped. You shall have a quiet Christmas indeed."

CHAPTER NINETEEN

"Thank you for coming with me." Emma reached over a gloved hand and grasped Millie's.

Millie eyed the contrast between the beautiful dyed pink leather and her own plain brown gloves and gave Emma's fingers a squeeze. The carriage moved with ease out of London, the hour early enough that the roads were quiet, the only traffic that of the merchants and delivery services.

Once they reached the less well-maintained roads, however, the mud caused by the tiny flurries of snow and frequent bouts of rain made progress much, much slower. By Millie's estimation, they moved no more than a mile in two hours, and though she tried to keep her expression calm, the tension in the closed carriage was palpable. If her heart beat fast, how rapidly did Emma's pound? If they did not get her to the coast, she would be wed to the duke in three days' time.

Emma rested her head against the plush cushion tucked at the side of her. "I cannot believe it has come to this."

"You wait," Millie said. "We shall find something on Westwick and as soon as his hold over you and Gabriel is over, you can return."

Emma bit down on her bottom lip. "If I do not leave, I fear Gabriel will do something foolish, but to leave my daughter..." Her voice cracked and she turned away to peer out of the window.

"I know," she said softly but the truth was, she could not know. Even imagining such a situation could not summon the pain Emma must be feeling.

Inhaling audibly, Emma straightened in her seat. "Gabriel is the best of brothers. I cannot let him do something dangerous."

Millie nodded slowly. The thought of Gabriel doing something reckless made nausea rise in her throat but she could not confess that to his sister now could she?

"He fought a duel for me you know."

"He made mention of that."

Emma's dark brows lifted. "He did? I am surprised. That is one of the secrets the duke holds against him." She smiled briefly. "Though, he does trust you so."

She shifted in her seat. "He did not discuss the

exact details. I do not have any information I could use against him."

"Not that I expect you would!" Emma exclaimed hastily. "I trust you implicitly, naturally. But the whole situation was Westwick's fault anyway."

"Because of what he did do to you," she said softly.

"Well, that, and...he made Gabriel believe another man had..." Her throat bobbed. "I did not tell Gabriel of what happened for fear of what he might do but Westwick convinced him that another man had dishonored me. The man was a cad and a drunk, and frankly, cut from the same cloth as Westwick. I do not doubt he behaved just as the duke does, but he did nothing to me."

"So Gabriel dueled the wrong man? But surely the man said something?"

Emma lifted a shoulder. "I believe the man did not know if he had done it or not. So deep in his cups was he, that such an act seemed likely."

"How awful."

"I wish Gabriel had told me but it was too late. The man was dead and it was then I told of Westwick and his actions. Of course, by then, Gabriel had participated in an illegal duel and killed a man."

Millie shook her head sadly. Naturally, Gabriel had rushed to his sister's defense just as he had barreled into battle. What a dreadful situation.

"So Westwick essentially arranged for your brother to kill a man?"

"The man knows no honor."

"He does not."

The slow rattle of the carriage wheels peppered the silence. The fact Gabriel had killed a man in such a manner did not change her estimation of him. If anything, it relieved her. He'd still behaved with honor, unlike the duke.

"His fiancée didn't know exactly what had happened but she called off the engagement after that."

Her heart gave a sharp jolt and she whipped her head around. "Fiancée?"

"Oh yes. I mean he is a viscount and after his first engagement fell through he sought another wife."

"Another?" Millie's chest tightened. He'd had not just one but two? How did she not even know this?

"I thought you knew." Emma grimaced. "It wounded Gabriel, even if he would not admit it."

"He loved them?"

"Oh no." Emma shook her head. "They were to be marriages of convenience. His first fiancée, Jane, could not even bear to look upon him when he returned from the war. His next...well, I think she agreed to wed him for his title but she was not strong enough to deal with Gabriel." Her lips curved. "Unlike some other women..."

"There are more?"

"No, silly." Emma nudged her with an elbow. "You, of course."

Millie narrowed her gaze at the young woman. "Whatever do you mean?"

"I am no fool, Millie. I see how you two look at each other. Gabriel never looked at either of those women in such a manner. And you were kidnapped by him! If anyone has a reason to loathe him, it is you, yet you do not."

Millie twisted her hands together and eyed them. "I'm not sure what you mean."

"Yes you do," Emma insisted. "Why do you think I am telling you all of this if not to ensure there are no secrets between you and my brother? Now you will be free to—"

The carriage came to a sharp jolt, making them both rock forward. Millie put a hand to Emma's arm.

"What is it?"

Pressing her face to the window, she peered out and sucked in a sharp breath.

"Highwaymen."

"This Kidnap Club?"

Millie shook her head. "No."

"Then what do they want?"

Working quickly on the lace around her neck, she handed her hat to Emma who eyed it as though it was a hideous creature. Which, compared to Emma's velvet hat, it likely was. But there was no time to think on such matters.

"Give me your hat," she ordered, unbuttoning her coat. "And your pelisse."

"Millie?"

"Either they are here for coin or for you."

Millie sucked in a sharp breath. "The duke?"

"If they are here for you..." She took the velvet hat and placed it squarely on her head then shucked out of her coat and snatched Emma's. "Well, they can have me instead."

✻ ✻ ✻

The bitter taste in Gabriel's mouth tightened around his throat at the sound of horse hooves approaching the house. Something had gone wrong.

Maybe the roads were too bad. Perhaps a wheel had fallen off the carriage...

When he marched outside and spotted Emma, alone on horseback, the noose of terror tightened. No blow to the ribs from that damned Bishop could feel as bad as realizing Millie wasn't with her.

"What happened?" he demanded of his sister when she jumped from the horse.

"Millie," she said breathlessly as she handed the reins to a stable hand. "She's been taken."

He scowled. "Taken?"

"Highwaymen..." She paused, bent double and gulped down a breath. "They took her. They thought they were taking me, but they took her."

Only when he paused to take a proper look at

his sister did he realize she wore Millie's coat and hat. Had the damned woman disguised herself as his sister?

"It wasn't the Kidnap Club?"

Emma shook her head vigorously. "They took her at gunpoint—two men. Most certainly not the Kidnap Club." Her chin trembled. "Gabriel, they were aggressive, and I fear for her safety. I'm faster than Mr. Wells so I took Red and came as fast as I could."

He glanced at the lone horse and gave his sister a pat on the shoulder. "Where were you set upon?"

"Just past the quarter mile marker for Sutton. At a crossroads."

Well, it certainly couldn't be the Kidnap Club then. They hadn't planned to take her until past the small town. He couldn't say for certain, but he had a suspicion Westwick was in on this. Highwaymen hardly frequented the roads during the depths of winter—it wasn't worth it. Perhaps his man Bishop had figured out he planned to get his sister out of the country.

Whatever the reason for Millie's kidnapping, he needed to get to her. Now. If they realized they'd taken the wrong woman, any person hired by Bishop would have no qualms about disposing of her.

"Red will manage the journey," Emma said. "But, Gabriel, please be careful. They were rough sorts." She shook her head. "If I had realized what

Millie intended..."

"She would never have let you be taken," he assured his sister as he mounted the horse.

"Gabriel, should you not take a weapon?"

He shook his head. Pistols were a danger to the owner and anyone in the vicinity half the time. Give him a rifle any day. Besides, he did not want to waste precious time marching through the house and grabbing a dueling pistol and shot.

"I'll be back soon," he assured his sister and tugged on the reins.

True to his sister's word, Red moved as swiftly as the roads would allow, apparently enjoying the speedy pace after the struggle of pulling a carriage along muddy roads. He came upon the carriage just outside of the village of Sutton, as promised.

The driver grimaced. "They took Miss Strong, my lord. I tried to stop them but—"

Gabriel held up a hand. "In which direction did they go? They cannot have gone too far if I know anything of Miss Strong."

With the rutted, almost impassable roads, moving a kidnapped woman quietly would not be easy, and if they thought her his sister, they would be keeping her somewhere—either to ransom or to hand over to Westwick. He would wager the latter.

Wells motioned down a winding lane, edged by tall hawthorn hedges. "I followed on foot but lost sight of them past that farmhouse there."

"I won't be long," he declared, moving the

horse in the direction of the farmhouse and spurring her on.

He observed the building as he neared and spied no movement, burning lamps, or signs of forced entry at the doors. Whoever took her would be a fool to hold her so close by though whether Bishop would have managed to hire men of sense at this time of year who was to say. Each arched mark of fresh horse hooves in the mud had him convinced they'd continued on, however.

Slowing his pace, he concentrated on following the tracks until the road divided into two. He smiled grimly to himself. The tracks curved left with no sign of any others to the right. He'd wager his viscountcy on them having taken her to a barn not far ahead.

He left Red a little way from the building, tying him upon a tree branch, and approached on foot, his heart kicking into a fierce beat when he heard male voices. He inched around the ramshackle barn to the entrance way and looked around the corner of the brick wall.

The sight of Millie, bound by her hands and feet, sitting on a stool, with a rag in her mouth made his gut tighten. He'd already put her through enough. He couldn't let her suffer any longer.

The two men paced about the empty barn. The tall, skinny one paused to gesture at Millie. "She don't act like a lord's sister," he muttered.

"Well, she dresses like one," the second man

said, his face obscured by a large-brimmed hat as he tugged off a glove and studied his hand. "She bites like a bloody dog, though."

Gabriel allowed himself a smile. At least he wasn't the only kidnapper on the receiving end of her fighting spirit.

He spotted one gun, currently discarded upon a practically rotten table, one leg missing and replaced by an old mill stone, and quite far from the men. They could have another, but he doubted it. Weapons were not cheap and neither of these men looked to have much from their clothing and tired appearance.

Now was his chance.

He strode into the building and placed himself between the men and the table. Millie gave a little squeak, her eyes widening, and both men whirled to eye him.

"Who the devil are you?" asked the man in the floppy hat, eyeing him as though he'd walked in wearing nothing but a cravat.

"I want to purchase her from you." He folded his arms and adopted a posture that brokered no argument as to whether he should be in the barn or not.

"She's not for sale," replied the other man, "and you'd better leave or we'll—" His gaze landed on the pistol, and he clapped a hand across the back of his friend's head, knocking the hat to the floor and revealing a shock of white hair. "The gun, you dolt."

"We can settle this peacefully," Gabriel offered. "Ten pounds for the woman."

"We're getting paid twenty," countered the now hatless man.

"Idiot!" exclaimed his friend. "What if he's law?"

"Do I look like law?" Gabriel motioned up and down himself.

The infuriated man looked him over with a begrudging expression. There was one thing to be said for his scars—he certainly did not look much like a viscount or a bailiff or judge.

He quickly calculated the money he carried upon his person. "I'll pay you fifty," Gabriel offered.

Even Millie gave a squeak of surprise.

The white-haired man shared a look with his friend. "Bishop will kill us."

Bishop. Of course. Gabriel's instincts had been right. He must have been watching them as much as they'd been trying to watch him. "He'll have to catch you first. Fifty pounds will take you a long way from him."

"What guarantee do we have you'll pay?" the apparently cleverer one demanded.

He slipped a hand into his inner pocket and slowly pulled out five ten-pound notes, leaving his other hand raised. "You can have the money here and now."

"Bishop will be here soon," the white-haired man reminded his friend.

"So you should make your decision quickly," Gabriel urged.

He blew out a breath as both men hesitated. He didn't have much desire to meet with Bishop, as much as he'd like to kill the man for putting his sister and Millie in danger. Bishop would arrive alone but likely armed and would recognize Millie instantly. He'd rather die than put Millie in danger.

"Do you want the money or not?" he demanded. He fished his pocket watch out with his free hand and held it out. "You can have this too. Worth a large sum."

Both men's eyes widened, and the white-haired man took a closer look. "Looks real," he told his friend.

"So?"

They shared a look, eyed Millie, and both nodded.

"Free her first," Gabriel ordered.

"Money first." The tall man used a hand to hold his friend back.

Gabriel tossed the pocket watch at him and he scrabbled to snatch it. "If you want the fifty pounds, untie her."

His friend wasted no time scarpering over, untying her legs and hands then removing the rag across her mouth with caution, stepping swiftly back as though she might tear him to shreds at any moment.

"Loathsome, foul-breathed snake," she muttered before hastening to Gabriel.

The tall man blocked her way, his palm open. "The money."

With a smirk, Gabriel flung the money to the right, snatched Millie's arm and left the men to claw at the money. He shoved Millie onto the horse, mounted behind her, and moved swiftly in the direction of the carriage, only allowing himself a deep breath when he spotted the carriage and Wells.

"You need to stop being kidnapped," he told Millie.

"You paid fifty pounds," she exclaimed. "Fifty pounds!"

"And a pocket watch," he reminded her.

"How much was that worth?"

"You do *not* want to know."

"Good Lord," she muttered. "Fifty pounds and a pocket watch. Gabriel, that's so much money."

He drew her close to his chest. "Worth it," he told her softly and allowed himself a smile when she relaxed against him.

CHAPTER TWENTY

When Gabriel strode into the back of the empty shop, Millie's heart skipped a beat and her head felt as though it was full of wool. She couldn't forget his determination yesterday, the way he'd looked at her as though she was something precious that he could not lose. How he'd been willing to pay any amount for her. She swallowed hard when he pushed past the piles of fabric, his expression almost as determined as yesterday.

"How is Emma? We have so little time."

"How is my sister? Millie, she suffered no more than worrying for your fate." Gabriel scrubbed a hand through his hair. "I am more concerned about you."

"Me?" She pressed a hand to her chest. "Why

should there be anything wrong?"

"You were kidnapped if you recall." His expression was oddly dark when he stepped toward her and she backed up until two crates blocked her way.

The air about them felt thick with...something. They had scarcely had a moment together yesterday, Emma fussing over her upon her return and then Marcus Russell arriving when he realized Emma was no longer on the road.

"I was kidnapped before, if you recall." She tried to add lightness to her tone and failed.

"This was a *real* kidnapping."

"Well, I did not know the last one was not real," she pointed out, even managing to add a tiny smile at the end of the statement but it felt strained, wobbling on her lips when he closed the gap between them so that they were no more than a foot apart.

"Do you have any idea how much I..." He huffed out a breath. "Dear God, Millie, when Emma told me what happened..."

"Yes?"

His gaze met hers. "I felt like I might be dying."

"Oh," she managed to say after several painful heartbeats.

Was it possible for this brave, wonderful man to care for her welfare so deeply? The fate of a shopgirl had very few consequences to anyone save from her mother and a few friends. No one would write of her in the newspapers or talk of her kidnapping as they would have done with Emma.

But Gabriel's pained expression told her he cared. Maybe he'd even continue to care.

His jaw ticked. His gaze searched hers. She felt on a cliff's edge, ready to take the leap but held back by one thread. She needed to cut it but could she? If she put her fate in the hands of a nobleman, she could well end up like her mother with history repeating itself.

When she searched his expression, though, she could not find any reason not to give herself entirely up to him. Gabriel was nothing like Westwick. He himself admitted he barely fit into the role of nobleman. In some ways, she felt the same about her life. Being a mere shopgirl had never been enough for her, just as Gabriel could not simply sit aside and let life as a rich, indolent lord take its place. It was as though she saw an echo of herself in him and if they were together, the little gaps in her soul would be full, leaving her entirely whole.

Could she do the same for him? Lord knew, she wanted to.

He made the first move, bringing a finger up to touch her face, following it by his whole hand when she broke the thread and leaned into the touch.

She closed her eyes briefly and savored the warmth of his hand upon her cheek. "Oh, Gabriel," she murmured.

"I wish we had met under different circumstances. I would make you promises, but this problem of my sister..."

"I do not need any."

"You deserve them, Millie. You deserve to be treated far better than any of this."

Slowly, she placed her hands on his chest, flattening her fingers against the hard warmth of him and looking up at him. His hand moved to her shoulder and he followed it with his other one, effectively holding her captive while he fixed her with a firm look.

"If circumstances changed, if I could free her with ease, I would make you mine. You know that do you not?"

Her throat tight, she nodded. The words were unnecessary. Of course Gabriel would do nothing to dishonor her. He was incapable of such things. The thought of being his, however, made her head swirl as though she had drunk too much brandy. The promises—no matter how impossible they were at present—made her whole body flush with heat.

"Millie—"

"Just kiss me," she demanded. She couldn't stand any more talk of a future unknown. Right now, she wanted to experience the present. With him.

With a resigned groan, he dropped his head and pressed his mouth to hers in a sudden rush. The heat of his mouth overwhelmed her, shutting down any lingering thoughts, snapping the tiny thread of her control. She wound her hands up around his neck and flattened her body to his as he groaned in response and bundled her closer.

His thighs were hard against hers, her chest crushed to him. He was everywhere, in the firmness of his palms, the commanding touch of his mouth, the fingers now winding in her hair then down, down to her skirts where he bunched them, letting cool air touch the tops of her thighs. Thank goodness they were entirely alone.

His tongue tangled with hers, leaving her gasping for breath. Millie could think of nothing more than the next kiss, the next touch. Whether the future held anything for them or not, she knew what she wanted.

Him.

All of him.

"Gabriel..." she managed to whisper between kisses. "I can be yours. At least for this evening."

His throat bobbed when he moved back to eye her. Her heart gave a sickening thud. For an awful moment, she thought he might deny her, might turn away, and let his honor guide him, but it seemed the pull between them was too much.

His mouth met hers in a fierce, commanding rush, and Mille knew, whatever happened, things would never be the same for her again.

***

Gabriel could scarcely bring himself to wince when her hand brushed his scarred face. When Millie kissed him, he forgot all about them. He might only have one eye but he saw her well enough—saw her flushed cheeks, her kiss-bruised lips, her heavy eyelids, and the way she looked at him as though he might well be the most wonderful man in the world.

When she touched him, he almost believed it.

She ran a hand between them, kissing him furiously as she fought with the buttons of his waistcoat. Whilst she dealt with that, he shucked off his jacket and pushed her gown from her shoulder, revealing the line of her stays and some sweet, pale skin.

He laid a kiss there then moved his lips up to her neck, as he caressed her breast through her garments. She was delicate, vulnerable—so unlike the Millie he knew. How he longed to bundle her up and keep her protected from everything.

But if things turned out the way he expected them to, he wouldn't be here to protect her.

The thought only briefly interrupted the pleasure of having her in his arms. It flittered away like a tiny snowflake on a breeze, leaving nothing but the faintest tingle of an impression. Her hands trailed a path down his shirt and tugged at the few buttons there before she slipped her fingers into the gap. He pressed a breath between his teeth.

"Dear God, woman."

"Take it off," she demanded.

He hesitated briefly. The scars on his body were minimal compared to that of his face so why they should give him pause, he did not know, but no one had seen them save for the those who had nursed him back to health.

"Gabriel," she pressed, tugging the cambric shirt, and biting on her bottom lip.

The building ache inside him grew agonizing. His cock threatened to burst free of his trousers and now he felt like his damned shirt was strangling him. He pulled it off so quickly Millie eyed him with amusement until he flung it behind him, likely lost amongst the piles of fabric forever. He didn't care. Not when she looked at him with a hunger that somehow made his arousal bigger than ever. If he'd had doubts about her attraction to him, they were long gone.

"Oh, Gabriel." She splayed her fingers across him, touched the scars briefly, then met his gaze. "You surely deserve your angelic name."

He smirked. "Oh yes, many would agree with you," he said dryly.

"You are beautiful."

He shook his head and cupped her face in one hand. "No. This...this is beauty." He kissed her lips. "These lips are made for kissing, and these cheeks..." He kissed each one. "These eyes...I swear I can think of nothing but you when you look at me." He pressed his mouth to her closed lids. "This neck too...never has there been a more beautiful, kissable neck." When he laid kisses down the arch of her skin, she shivered. "You are perfection," he told her sincerely when he found her mouth again.

Any further words were forgotten, lost to action, as he deepened the kiss and held her close to his bare chest. She moved against his arousal, causing blissful pleasure mingled with pain. He wanted nothing more than to be joined with her, to know she was his, but he needed more of her first. If he was never going to do this again, it had to be...everything.

Hands to her waist, he moved her back, shoved ledgers and wool to the floor then lifted her onto the table. She reached for him but he ducked her hands, instead dropping to his knees.

Her eyes widened. "What are you...?"

"Has anyone ever kissed you here?"

"No, of course not!"

When he lifted her skirts and shoved them up her thighs, he caught the musky smell of her and bit back a groan. Her protests vanished as he kissed his way up her thighs then found the sweet apex.

He gave her a bold stroke of his tongue and she cried out, her short nails digging into his shoulders. Once she'd eased into his ministrations, he swirled and nibbled and licked, alternating gentle touches between more vigorous ones. Her legs tightened around his head, her body trembling. He licked and sucked until her hips bucked to meet his kisses and her whole body tensed. She pulsed beneath his tongue and gasped out his name. He waited a few moments and dropped a few gentle kisses upon her skin before rising.

Her cheeks were rosy-red and she gripped the edge of the table. "Gabriel, that was…" She put a hand to her chest. "I did not know…"

He took her face in both hands, lifting her chin. "Millie, are you an innocent?" he asked, wondering why the hell he'd never asked before.

She nodded, then gripped his arms. "But it does not matter. I want you, Gabriel, more than anything in the world. I do not need to be experienced to know that. I…I love you."

He searched her expression, seeing nothing that could give him doubt. When had Millie ever done anything she did not wish to do. She reached for him, cupping his aching cock in her palm, and he closed his eyes.

"How much…" He grunted when she moved her palm again. "How much do you know of the act?"

"Enough."

He opened his eyes to spot the confident lift of her chin. Hell, how could he deny her? Especially when she kept doing…dear God…that to him.

Removing her hand, he moved between her thighs. "Keep doing that and we won't even get to the act."

"Kiss me."

"As you bid," he said with a tilted smile.

He claimed her mouth and cupped a breast, grateful for undergarments that weren't made of rigid boning or stiff fabrics as he teased a thumb over her hard nipple and heard her gasped responses. Then he clasped the back of her neck so he could watch when he slid a hand between her thighs to play his fingers over her folds. Gratification surged through him when she gasped and her eyes widened.

"Again?" she asked.

"Again."

Millie rocked against his hand, moving with his ministrations and when he finally slipped a finger between her folds, she shivered. He held her close to him, his breaths ruffling her hair as he worked her to a climax. She slumped her head against his shoulder, and he couldn't help but smile. Right now, he could probably die a happy man.

"Whatever are you doing?"

He frowned.

She put a finger to his mouth, tracing it. "I've never seen this smile before."

"That's because I have never seen you climax before."

"Well, now you have."

"And I will again," he vowed.

"Oh...good..."

When he kissed her this time, any control he had fled. She clawed at him like a wild woman, as desperate as he to be joined together. He fumbled with the rest of his clothes, shoving them down around his thighs and tilting his head back when she curled cool fingers around him. He allowed only the tiniest exploration, his jaw tight, then he parted her thighs and brushed against the heat of her with a moan.

"You are certain?" he paused to ask.

She nodded vigorously.

Gabriel eased into her, every muscle in his body tight as she gave way to him. Once joined fully with her, he released a breath, and pressed his forehead to hers while he took in the sensations. Never before had he felt so complete, so damned content.

What a shame this would be fleeting. He swore he could spend the rest of the day—or the rest of his life—making love to this woman.

A hand to her thigh and the other to her hip, he moved slowly then increased the pace as her body relaxed around him. The moment for softness and caution fled when she tipped her head back, her hair spilling down her back. He pressed erratic kisses to her face, her neck and thrust into her.

Pleasure built, burning through him, making the hairs on his arms stand on end. Her body pulsed around him, so so close. All he had to do was press a hand between them, touch her lightly and she exploded, taking him with her. He thrust once, twice, a third time, slamming into her, and withdrew hastily to spill on her thigh.

He gulped down heavy breaths and moved a hand to the back of her neck to hold her against him. He'd wanted more. He longed to remain inside her, take the chance she would bear his child and become a viscountess.

But to save Emma, he knew what he had to do, and that meant no chance of a future for them, no matter how much he loved this woman.

CHAPTER
TWENTY-ONE

T he thin white blanket of snow could not take away from the dreariness of the stone building, tinged in gray from smoke and dirt. Tattered curtains hung in the window of the lower lodgings and no lamps were lit, despite thick clouds hanging over London, threatening another coat of snow. Millie wrapped an arm about herself and shivered, uncertain if it was due to the cold or the grimness of the accommodations.

Or perhaps due to the fact they were running out of time. In mere days, Emma would be wed. She'd seen the inevitability in Gabriel's grim expression this morning and despite being surrounded by most of the members of the Kidnap Club, she'd longed to put her arms about him and absorb some of the pain etched into his scarred face.

Embraces would have to wait, though. As would anything between them. For now, Emma was their focus, especially considering they could no longer get her to Ireland with the awful weather. Roads were practically impassable and they wouldn't get anywhere fast on foot.

She rapped her knuckles against the door and spied movement behind the curtains. She kept her head lowered into the warmth of her scarf, partly to fend off the cold, partly to look as unthreatening as possible. Gabriel had not had much luck speaking with some of the duke's former servants and it seemed it wasn't just because of his appearance. Even the exceedingly persuasive Rosamunde had struggled to get information on Westwick. Years after being in his employ, maids and butlers alike were still terrified of him.

It stood to reason there had to be something they could use against him. A man with such a reputation could not have gone through this life without leaving some sort of trail. But how they would find that thread, she did not know. All of them were scrambling to find something now.

Gabriel had gone to a gaming hell that Bishop was known to frequent, Russell was digging into something sordid that he refused to talk about in front of the women, and Guy and Nash were at the gentlemen's clubs, subtly inquiring about various financial speculations the duke had partaken in. As far as she knew, Grace had her hands on some old correspondence of the duke's and was digging her way through that while the other women were doing the same as her. Even Lucy had left her shop early to help.

She blew out a breath that misted in front of her. It might all be for nought.

The door opened slowly and a thin woman peered up at her from a hunched position. Dark gray hair streaked with lines of paler gray was pulled back into a severe chignon, leaving her scalp so tight her eyebrows were lifted in a permanently surprised expression. Her lips were tightly pursed, surrounded by the sort of wrinkles that made one appear as though she had sucked on something sour.

"Are you Mrs. Parsons?" Millie asked.

"I am."

"I was hoping to speak to you about Westwick."

Her brow furrowed, barely moving the frozen eyebrows. "I haven't heard that name in a long time."

Considering the duke resided in London for much of the year, Millie wasn't sure how to respond to that. Perhaps the woman did not associate with many people or read the scandal sheets.

"But I'm busy," she said and turned to shut the door.

Millie put a hand to the door and lifted the basket she'd brought with her. "I have a parcel."

The woman's eyes narrowed in on the covered

basket. Underneath, she would find a carefully packed bundle from Emma. The offerings were a last attempt at getting people to talk of the duke and it seemed it worked on Mrs. Parsons.

"Did Westwick send you?" She smiled, revealing uneven and missing teeth. "He always was a good boy."

"I come from a wealthy family who wish to spread the joy at Christmas," Millie said vaguely, wondering if it was possible a man like Westwick had ever had a good bone in his body.

"Ah, I knew he had not forgotten me."

Millie didn't correct her as the woman ushered her into a parlor room that smelled of must and tobacco smoke. She spied a clay pipe resting upon a tray on a table next to a worn armchair. The wallpaper peeled in places and the floorboards underfoot creaked, barely covered by a tattered rug in front of a dying fire. If Westwick was as good a man as she said, clearly his care did not extend to ensuring his old nanny was looked after in her retirement.

The woman sat in the armchair and reached out using grabbing motions for the basket. Millie blinked, set it in her hands and sat opposite her when no further invitations came. The woman delved into the basket, drawing out a set of knitted gloves, a carefully wrapped pudding, and a tin of sweetmeats with a cackle. "Such a good boy."

"Westwick?"

"Oh yes." She popped open the tin lid, took out a marzipan and closed her eyes while she sucked on it.

"I would love to hear about your time raising him."

The woman's eyes opened and she sighed. "It has been many years. Once the boys were under the tutelage of their school master, I was no longer needed and goodness knows, the then Westwick wasn't going to go near his wife to sire anymore children."

"What was Westwick like? You said he was a good child?"

"Oh the best." She smiled softly. "Such a patient baby." Her expression soured and she snapped the lid of the tin shut then set it onto the table next to the pipe. "Unlike his brother."

"Westwick had a twin brother, did he not?"

"Indeed and the child might well have been born from the devil himself. "

"Oh? He was a bad child?"

"Oh yes that too, but the wretched thing refused to use his right hand." She leaned in close. "Always favored his left." Mrs. Parsons jabbed a sharp finger at her. "Mark of the devil that is. Good job he died or we'd have the devil walking amongst us."

"Oh yes," Millie agreed vaguely. "That would be awful."

The woman muttered on about how wonderful Westwick was for what felt like an eternity. Stories of a child so sweet and innocent made Millie wonder what on earth had happened to him to change him so much. Mrs. Parsons finished all the sweetmeats before Millie left, gleefully sucking them down as she reminded Millie over and over to thank Westwick for his charity.

Snow fell in thick chunks by the time she'd reached her new shop, seeping through her outer garments. She paused, shoved a damp strand of hair from her face, and frowned at a printed letter nailed firmly to the front door. She tore it from the nail and scanned the bold headline.

SHOP HERE AND DEAL WITH THE DEVILE.

Beneath it was a description of the supposed acts she had partaken in, many too lurid for even the most imaginative of people to conjure. She peered up and down the road, her stomach twisted into knots. How many people had seen this? How many would never return? It was all lies, of course, but it wouldn't matter—some damage might well be done to her reputation as a shop owner.

She shoved the letter into her cloak pocket and tugged the nail but it remained embedded firmly in the front door. Somehow, she suspected this would not be the last time this happened and she knew exactly who was behind trying to tarnish her reputation, but without any new information on the duke, what could she even do about it? The whole situation was feeling more hopeless by the second.

***

Gabriel barged past the stony-faced butler who apparently decided he wasn't worth the effort. The man shrank back against the wall. He supposed there were some benefits to looking like a monster. He felt like one at the moment. The anger burned through him, so hot he feared he'd explode. His pulse beat hard in his fingertips and no amount of snow could douse the fire. He didn't bother removing his hat or outer garments as he stormed through the house, briefly stopping to demand where the master was from a maid.

She eyed him in horror, pointing a trembling finger toward double doors. Gabriel stalked over, pushed them apart, and shoved them shut behind him when he spied Westwick.

The man had the gall to smirk. Gabriel balled his hands into fists and reminded himself the man would be dead before long—and it was far better to ensure he was dead in an honorable manner, though the desire to ram a fist into the man's face until that smirk was well and truly gone made his fingers flex so he tightened them again.

"What is the meaning of this?" He tossed the letter into Westwick's lap.

He slowly closed the book in his lap, set it aside and eyed the crumpled letter. "Someone seems to have revenge in mind. But what does this have to do with me?"

"This business is between you and me, do you understand? You leave Miss Strong out of this."

The duke rose as though he had all the time in the world. "Come now, we shall be brothers before long. Can we not make peace?"

"There can be no peace when you threaten others. She's your daughter for Godsakes."

His lip curled. "I only have her mother's word for that. Many a whore has tried to milk me for coin with such declarations."

Gabriel clamped his teeth together so hard they hurt. Millie's mother was a lovely woman and such words only made his determination for the man to see justice burn brighter.

"You had my sister kidnapped," Gabriel stated.

"I have no idea what you are talking about, Thornbury."

"The kidnappers were hired by your man."

Westwick shrugged. "What Bishop does in his own time is none of my business. Perhaps he thought it imperative to ensure my bride remains safe and secure in London." A languid smile crossed his lips. "But, I must wonder, why was Emma travelling at such a time? The roads are practically impassable and she might not have returned in time for the wedding. Have you forgotten everything I know of you and your family?"

"I've forgotten nothing," Gabriel spat, "but I am tired of your underhanded behavior, Westwick. You will not touch Miss Strong again."

His smile grew. "How fond you seem to be of this woman. Slumming it with a shopkeeper eh? I imagine none of the fine ladies of the *ton* wish to go near such a face."

Gabriel ignored the slight. His face, his fiancées, they meant little now, especially when he had the love of a woman like Millie. But this man...he was too dangerous, and he'd threatened Millie's dreams. He'd known this would have to come to an end soon, that their hopes of bringing the man down in a legal manner were slipping, but his threats toward Millie meant he could no longer wait. For his sister's and Millie's sake, Westwick had to die.

"A duel." Gabriel slowly tugged the fingers of his glove off one hand.

Westwick frowned. "I beg your pardon?"

"A duel, Westwick. Tomorrow. At a place of your choosing." Gabriel removed the glove and slapped it across Westwick's face, the sound ringing through the grand library. "Or are you too cowardly to face me like a gentleman?"

"Ha! A gentleman? You are barely a viscount. It was meant to be your brother's position and here you challenge a duke as though you shall not face consequences for the act?"

Gabriel lifted his shoulders. He would, and he didn't care, so long as not a breath was left in Westwick's body. The scandal of a trial and subsequent hanging would not be wonderful for Emma but he intended to ensure she had the support of the earl and his friends as well as Millie.

Millie.

The thought of leaving her made his throat tighten. That would be worst of all, though he was certain she would understand. Did she not always wish to help others? She'd offered to help him for Christ's sake when he most certainly did not deserve it. He'd ensure she was set up well for the future, however, so she could continue to make a success of her business and look after her mother.

"Are you too cowardly to face me, Westwick?" he demanded when the duke remained silent.

Westwick lifted his chin and met Gabriel's hard stare. "Of course not. Tomorrow it is then. I'll send word of when and where." He glanced at the paper in his hand and flung it into the fireplace. "I'll arrange a physician but be warned, Thornbury, he won't be interested in tending to a mere viscount."

Gabriel didn't care. He wouldn't die anyway. There were few men who were a better shot than he but he never boasted about it. A fine thing too, considering his shot would be perfect tomorrow.

CHAPTER TWENTY-TWO

Millie's heart scarcely had time to skip a beat when Gabriel strode into the rear of the shop, his brow furrowed, his stride determined. Her gasp was cut off when he took her face in his hands, pressed a blistering kiss to her mouth that left her wanting, then pressed his forehead to hers.

"What was that for?" she managed to utter through a tight throat, aware Betsy and several customers milled about the shop only feet from them and a quick glance into the open door would reveal her and Gabriel.

"I love you," he said.

"I love you too." The words were husky.

"I always will. No matter what happens, never forget that."

She drew back from his hold but took his arms in her hands. "No matter what? Gabriel, I—" She searched his face. "If this is about Emma, we still have four days. We shall put a stop to this wedding. The Kidnap Club is working hard on the matter."

His jaw twitched. "I just need you to know, Millie."

She smiled when he rubbed a gloved finger across her cheek. "I know."

"Good." He glanced around the storeroom. "Will the new shop open tomorrow as planned?"

"I am a little behind, no thanks to a certain someone," she teased. "But it shall happen. I shall simply have to move the rest of my stock over the next few evenings but the shop is ready enough."

"I wish I could be there but—"

"You have your sister to worry about, Gabriel. I know if circumstances were different, you would be at my side."

He nodded stiffly, sighed, and stepped back. "I love you," he repeated, the words sounding slightly hollow and making her frown.

Before she could ask why, he ducked out of the room. Millie eased out a breath, folded her arms, and rested against one of the packed crates. Nausea rolled in her stomach but she could not be certain why. Gabriel loved her—surely that was cause for celebration? Something was strange about him, though, and the manner in which he'd spoken.

He'd been like...like...

Her heart rebounded hard against her chest. He'd been like a man saying farewell.

But why would he be saying such a thing to her?

Oh Lord. Was he going to do something reckless? Something that would ensure she would never see him again? Whatever it was she had to stop him,.

She snatched her cloak from the hat stand in the corner of the shop, smiling politely to a young woman and pausing to gain Betsy's attention with a wave while the assistant dealt with a regular customer of theirs.

"I just need to..." She didn't know what to say. *Run after a lord who is about to do a very silly thing I just do not know what?* It sounded preposterous. "I'll be back soon," she vowed.

With any luck she would talk Gabriel out of whatever it was and he would kiss her and this awful sickening feeling in her stomach would be gone.

"That's fine," Betsy said. "It's quiet today."

Mr. Humphries, a wide-set man with a gregarious smile and fashionable clothes grinned at them. "All ready for the new premises?"

"Indeed," Millie managed to agree as she tied her cloak about her neck and fought to stuff her hands into her gloves.

"I shall be sending Lilith for her trousseau before long and no doubt the girl shall cost me a

King's ransom."

Millie smiled tightly. Mr. Humphries was a generous man and would fulfil his promise but she didn't have time to talk with him.

"Will you sign here, sir?" Betsy asked of him, and he leaned plucked up the quill to sign his purchase in the ledger.

"Forgive me, I always smudge." He grimaced and lifted away an ink-stained hand. "My headmaster tried to beat it out of me but to no avail."

Millie paused, her glove halfway up her hand. "You are left-handed, Mr. Humphries?"

"I hope it does not offend. Goodness knows, I tried my whole childhood not to be but it is something one cannot help."

"Some say it is the mark of the devil..." she murmured.

"Unfortunately my headmaster agreed."

"Nonsense, I am certain," Betsy said, giving Millie a look.

"Oh yes," she said hastily, realizing how close she'd come to offending one of their best customers. "Utter nonsense. But quite a hassle, I see." She eyed the smudge on the page where Mr. Humphries had signed his name.

"Yes." He flashed his ink-stained hand at her. "Never could write without smudging."

Millie sucked in a sharp breath that seared her lungs. Westwick was left-handed. She'd seen his letters to her mother. But the nanny had said...

The nanny had said the younger twin was the left-handed child.

"I must dash," she managed to say before escaping the shop. Gabriel was long gone, no doubt having ridden or taken the carriage here, so she ducked her head against the bitter splashes of snowflakes and headed directly to his house. Her cheeks were painfully numb and her breaths came hard and fast by the time she reached the house but the butler let her in with a roll of his eyes and took her directly to Emma.

"Is Gabriel here?" Millie demanded.

Emma covered the distance between them. "No. Why?"

"Where has he gone?"

"To Westwick's. He seemed convinced he was going to be able to make a deal with the man and put a stop to the wedding." She shrugged. "I am not so certain but Gabriel promised me it would be over and you know my brother does not make promises lightly."

Millie fought to untangle the knot slowly tightening around her throat. Gabriel was going to put an end to this but not by way of negotiation, of that she was certain.

"I need to go to him."

Emma blinked, and her brow furrowed as she scanned Millie's expression. "Give me but a moment and I shall come too."

"No. I need you to get word to the Kidnap Club."

"Of what?"

"Westwick is not Westwick."

"Whatever do you mean?"

"Westwick…" Millie drew in a breath. "Is the younger twin. He is pretending to be his brother. He has taken his place."

A few moments passed then Millie's eyes widened. "You think he killed his brother? To take the dukedom from him?"

"Perhaps, though I cannot fathom why."

"Goodness me. No one would guess at such a thing. He would inherit after his brother's death anyway."

"I know." And she didn't have time to dwell on quite why Westwick had decided to follow such a ruse but from what little she knew of the older twin, it did not sound at all like the current Westwick. "Will you send word?"

Emma nodded vigorously. "Of course. I shall go immediately. But what shall you do?"

"I must go to your brother and inform him of what we know." Hopefully before it was too late.

***

Russell held the pistol back from Gabriel's reach. "Are you certain you wish to do this?"

Gabriel stared past him at Westwick, who offered a smug smile when he took his weapon from his second and gave a firm nod. "I have little other choice."

"Rosamunde is going to kill me when she realizes I'm involved in this duel."

"I appreciate you coming. I could ask no one else." Gabriel fixed him with a look. "I assume you've told no one."

The man nodded. "Naturally. As I said before, I cannot say I would not do the same in such a situation but you know where this will lead."

"I won't die."

Russell tilted his head slightly back and eyed him. "Not yet at least." He offered out the weapon and Gabriel curved his hand around the comforting weight of the gun. "Want me to try to negotiate again?"

"No."

"You'd better be a good shot." Russell gestured to his own eye. "Will that not hinder you? If the duke survives, your sister shall be no better off than she was before, except she will be without you to protect her."

"He won't survive," Gabriel said through gritted teeth. "And I might have lost a damned eye but I never lost my ability to shoot straight."

The large man shrugged. "I did not really expect otherwise, but I had to ask."

Gabriel eyed Russell for a few moments. Were it not for the fact he was about to shoot a duke, he would wager he and Marcus Russell would have continued to work well together in the future. The man had all the skills and courage of someone who had fought all his life to survive and Gabriel could not respect him more. He also knew Russell understood when one had to make a difficult decision and was the only man he could count on not to try to sway him out of this duel.

"I hope your wife forgives you," Gabriel told him.

"Oh she will eventually." He flashed a grin. "She doesn't know it but I understand well enough how to charm her."

"Let's get this bloody thing done," called Westwick. "I have better things to do with my time than shoot a cripple."

For once, Gabriel was grateful for the duke's arrogance. Had he understood how skilled Gabriel was with a pistol, there was no chance the man would have agreed to a duel. Westwick knew that if Gabriel died today, there would be no justice for Gabriel—his rank and wealth would ensure as much—so as far the duke was concerned he could not lose.

Well, he was about to discover his title and wealth could not save him today.

Westwick took up his position upon the open field. Russell gave Gabriel a reassuring nod and the seconds took a step back while the physician remained some distance away near a single oak tree. Gabriel inhaled deeply, wished he could have made love to Millie one last time, then started pacing.

One, two, three, four...

A scream ripped through the biting cold air. He

paused and twisted to spy Millie dashing across the field, skirts and the edge of her cloak gripped in one hand.

"Gabriel," she shouted. "Do not do it."

He lowered his head. She couldn't stop him now. Five, six, seven…

"Gabriel!"

He caught sight of her in the periphery of his vision, barreling past Russell's outstretched arms, right into the line of fire.

"Millie," he shouted as he twisted, flinging his weapon to the ground, and preparing to dash toward her. "Get out of the damned way." He spied Westwick raise his weapon. A shot rang out and Millie fell to the ground before he reached her.

He dropped to his knees, the gunshot still echoing in his ears, the thud of his heart so painful he felt it vibrate through every inch of his body.

"No," he heard himself say when he turned her over.

There was no blood. Where was the blood? He patted her arms, her torso, down her sides. She stared up at him, her cheeks red, then pushed up to sitting.

"You are not hurt."

"No, though it was deuced close." She put a finger to her ear and though her gloves were too dark to reveal blood, he saw the smear of it upon the shell of her ear.

He pressed a breath through his teeth. "Bloody

hell, Millie."

"Shall we go again seeing as the wench is alive?" called Westwick.

Gabriel narrowed his gaze at the duke, fist clenched. The man nearly killed the woman he loved, his own daughter, and it scarcely passed the duke's notice. He went to rise to his feet but Millie grabbed his arms, forcing him to remain upon his knees.

"You cannot duel him."

"I can and I will. He nearly killed you, Millie."

"No, you do not understand. He's not the duke."

Gabriel stopped trying to rise and scowled. "Not the duke?"

"Well, he is. But not the original duke. He's his brother," she hissed. "He's the younger twin. He's pretending to be his brother. He took his place."

For a few moments, he let the information sink in.

"He probably killed him," she added.

He eyed the duke then met Millie's pleading gaze. "It doesn't matter, I have to kill him. He's the duke now."

"No, you do not." She gripped his arms so tight, he'd wager her nails would leave marks in his arms. He hated to leave her, he really did, but regardless of this information, the world believed Westwick to be, well, Westwick, and nothing he knew would help Emma now.

"You cannot do this, Gabriel, please, I'm begging you."

"Millie…"

"Let me negotiate with him."

"Russell already has."

She swung a look at Russell that made Gabriel rather grateful he was not on the receiving end of it. Russell shrank back a few steps and Gabriel could not help but smile at the man being intimidated by Millie.

"No, let me negotiate with this new information," she begged. "If it does not work, you can go back to shooting him." She inhaled audibly. "With my blessing."

Gabriel touched her bloody ear and muttered a curse. "Very well, but you cannot get in the way this time. You must let me do this, Millie."

"So long as you let me do this."

"Together then."

CHAPTER TWENTY-THREE

Blood tinged Millie's gloves. She swiped them down her cloak and ignored the ringing in her ears. It had been so close. Too close. Gabriel could have died.

Well, she was going to put an end to this today without anyone having to die, even her wretched father. She marched toward Westwick and Bishop. If the duke had any remorse about nearly killing his own daughter, he did not reveal it. His lips were pulled into a smirk, his head tilted back with an air of arrogance.

From his side, Bishop eyed her as though he wished the bullet had gone through her *and* Gabriel and wiped them both from the earth.

"What the devil do you think you are playing at, girl?" Westwick demanded. "This is not a game

—this is business between men."

"This is no game," she agreed.

"Why do you not get out of the way and let us damned well finish."

"You will not be finishing anything, most especially your business with Gabriel."

He peered around her, his smirk growing. "Need a woman to fight for you now, Thornbury?" he taunted.

Millie stepped closer, rising onto tiptoes so he could not avoid her gaze. "I know what you did."

"I have done many things in my life, my dear. It is hard to recall them all."

"You killed your brother."

The briefest flicker of surprise made his lids flutter then he composed himself. She glanced at Bishop and could not help letting a smug smile cross her lips. It seemed his man knew of the act too. He shifted briefly on his feet and then clasped his hands behind his back, avoiding her gaze.

She shook her head. The arrogance of these men was so great that neither of them assumed anyone would discover their ruse.

"My brother died many years ago, in his sleep after a bout of illness. It was a most traumatic time," Westwick said with all the warmth of the icy day.

"Your brother was your identical twin, was he not?" Millie asked.

"I am not going to entertain these questions."

He waved a hand at her. "Are we to do this or not, Thornbury, or shall I just see you at St Paul's tomorrow?"

"You killed him because he was heir to the dukedom. I imagine you were getting worried he would wed soon and sire an heir, forgoing you entirely." She let her smile grow when his jaw tightened. "It must have rankled that your twin should get the title and you would not despite being born at the same time."

"You have no idea of what you are speaking, girl."

"I know that you are left-handed. I have written evidence. And that your twin—the true Westwick was right-handed. You killed him somehow and took his place, then wrote to my mother, as your brother, to end things with her. It would be easy to compare the two samples of handwriting she had. One from my true father, and one from you." She sucked in a breath. "And I know that your arrogance is so great that you never even attempted to learn to use your right hand to ensure the security of your ruse." She nodded toward Bishop. "From his expression, I imagine he aided you in some manner. I wonder if his loyalty would remain when it is revealed he killed a duke."

Westwick made a dismissive noise. "A fanciful story but do you really think anyone would be willing to risk my wrath to follow such accusations from a deranged and revengeful woman? Besides, why should I do such a thing? I was next in line anyway."

"I have the letter you wrote to my mother, and I have no doubt there is more evidence of your act. Perhaps you had a reputation you wished to escape —Mrs. Parsons said you were quite an awful child and amounted some debt in your adulthood. Much easier to simply become your brother who was much beloved maybe?"

His jaw ticked and she knew her assumptions were close to the truth and her furious heartbeat slowed a little.

"But do you not see, Westwick? You are one of the most powerful and known men in England. Such information would not go unnoticed, even if it was mere rumor."

He eyed her for several moments. "I should just kill you. Then finish this damned duel and kill this beast of a man you seem so determined to protect."

"You would have to kill the doctor and Mr. Russell too," she pointed out. "And you do not even have a bullet in your gun anymore. Do you think Gabriel would let you live if you did such a thing?"

His lips twitched. "You are certainly a Westwick."

Millie lifted her chin. "I am my mother's daughter, nothing more."

He stepped closer to her. "I could claim you, ensure you and your mother are wealthy and looked after. No one would question such a thing. Just rid yourself of those letters and you could have everything your heart desires."

She opened her mouth and closed it. She'd never felt the lack of a father in her life but it had certainly been a struggle to pull herself up from poverty. There had been days when she might well have done anything for a single meal.

But she'd done it properly and honestly, without help from a man who had likely never worked a day in his life.

She looked back at Gabriel, a lone figure in the snow, his posture pensive and his gaze fixed upon her, and she smiled.

"Westwick, I have everything my heart desires already."

The duke rolled his eyes. "Dear God, all this for a man with the face of a beast."

"At least he does not have the heart of one," she countered.

"I could still ruin you all. I could sue you for slander. And that man you adore so much is a killer too. Did you know that?"

"Westwick!" his man spluttered.

"A killer too? So you confess to the killing of your brother then?"

"Dash it all, shut up, Bishop." He stepped closer to her, his jaw tense. "I confess to nothing, you have nothing."

"I have enough and I shall have more. Unless you allow Emma to break off the engagement and never speak ill of either her or Lord Thornbury."

"I could make you vanish," he pressed through his teeth.

Millie met his cold stare and her stomach twisted. She had no doubt he'd made people disappear before, that his man had more than the blood of Westwick's brother on his hands.

"There are others and they know of your deeds. You will have to make a lot of important people vanish, Westwick."

He snorted. "Your threats mean nothing, girl."

"They mean something to me," a man called from behind Millie. She twisted and eased out a long breath. The Kidnap Club was here.

***

Westwick's posture stiffened when he spotted Lord Henleigh alongside Russell, Nash, and Lady Henleigh and Russell's wife Rosamunde. He had an audience now.

Gabriel could not help but smirk. He might not get the satisfaction of killing the man but there was a certain pleasure to be had in seeing the smugness fall from the man's face.

Guy handed Gabriel a letter and he frowned, eyeing the unfamiliar writing.

"You recall that lover you could not find?"

Gabriel nodded.

"Grace finally received word from her. It was written two weeks ago but the blasted roads probably ensured its delay."

Gabriel read the letter then strode over to Millie to hand it to her.

Westwick rolled his eyes. "If you think some letter is going to prove anything..."

"I thought this woman was yet another of your discarded lovers, but she was your brother's intended, was she not?" Gabriel glanced at Millie.

Westwick waved a dismissive hand. "I cannot recall every woman who falls at my damned feet."

"Perhaps you can recall the arranged marriage between the Duke of Westwick that was broken off when your brother wished to do the honorable thing."

"My brother died," Westwick hissed. "If he was going to wed—"

"He had a mistress and she was with child. He intended to marry her and you feared the child would be a boy and inherit," Gabriel continued, ignoring him. "Hence, why you ensured he did not survive long enough to wed her."

"This is all—"

"She says they were to marry but she knew the duke's heart was not in it, that he loved another. She broke off the engagement so he could marry another woman—a maid in his household." Millie waved the letter at him, her eyes misting. "He was to marry Miss Strong. My mother." The last word came out choked. Her chest rose as she drew in a breath. "This verifies everything I assumed." She jerked a head toward Bishop. "And it seems your man sent a few threats to your brother's fiancée, of which she still has record, in case she decided to tell anyone of your brother's intentions. She assumed it was to protect the family from scandal."

Behind him, Bishop twitched uncomfortably.

The rest of the group moved closer.

Freya folded her arms. "There is also the fact that your second wife and brother died in similar circumstances. Strange, considering neither you nor your brother were known for laudanum use. I found an old newspaper article suggesting your brother killed himself over his many debts. I wonder what would happen if it was suggested someone was responsible for both deaths..."

Bishop took a step back and Westwick rounded on him. "Don't you move, you bloody bastard. I have enough evidence on you—"

"Because you made me do these things, my lord," the man spluttered. "And I have evidence on you too."

Westwick's eyes rounded. "You would not dare."

"You threaten me, my lord, and I'll threaten you. I have evidence where you'll never find it." He met Gabriel's gaze. "And I'll give it all to them if I need to."

"You cowardly little s—"

Bishop ducked a swipe from Westwick and folded his arms, his expression a picture of insolence. Gabriel would never like Bishop—the man was heartless and likely had the blood of many innocents on his hands—but at least the man was clever enough to ensure he had protection. Westwick's posture sagged. It was all coming apart for him.

"None of this means anything." Westwick tilted his head back, adopting an impervious expression. "All of this is conjecture and I will sue for slander." He thrust a finger toward Freya.

Guy stepped in front of his wife, his jaw tight. "We know enough, Westwick."

"You killed your brother because you wanted the title," Millie said firmly. "And you threatened his fiancée. You took your brother's place—who was a fine and good man by the looks of it—to escape the foolish mistakes you made."

"I made no mistakes—" Westwick clamped his mouth shut.

Gabriel smirked. Their evidence was still scant but it was enough to have Westwick and his man falling apart. He had no doubt a little squeeze and Bishop would give up all the evidence he had.

"Will you allow Emma to end your betrothal?" Millie demanded.

His flinty gaze skipped from Millie's to Gabriel's for several moments then he took a step back and waved a dismissive hand at her. "Fine. Emma is released from our betrothal."

"And?"

"And I shall do my best to ensure she receives

no censure over the late decision," he muttered. "But if anything comes out about...this nonsense... I have your mistakes and that bastard child of Emma's..."

Gabriel tightened a fist. The arrogance of the man knew no bounds. He had killed a duke and yet thought nothing of threatening him and his sister. But the threats were said in trembled tones and Bishop kept inching away from the duke. It wouldn't take much for Westwick's deception to fall apart.

"Go and cancel the wedding," Gabriel ordered. "And if you go near my sister or any other woman for that matter, I will still happily take your life."

Westwick sniffed. "I never wanted the damned whore anyway."

Gabriel felt the sting in his knuckles before he quite realized what he'd done. Westwick staggered back several steps, a hand to his jaw. He gaped at Gabriel then gestured wildly to Bishop.

"Aren't you going to do anything about this insolence?"

Bishop shook his head vigorously, took several steps back, then dashed off over the fields. Gabriel cupped his hand and chuckled at the sight. With any luck, without the protection of the duke, Bishop would find life a lot harder now.

Russell clapped a hand over Gabriel's' shoulder. "Feel better now?"

Gabriel smiled, meeting the man's gaze, and

glancing around at all of them.

He looked to Millie. "Almost. But there is one more thing I need to do."

EPILOGUE

One year later

Millie gnawed on the end of her thumb and pushed up onto tiptoes to peer down the road. Snow fell in thick clumps, gradually building upon the windowsill and masking her view of the approach to the country house.

Firm hands latched around her arms and she whirled, her pulse kicking into a furious beat. She pressed a hand to her chest. "You startled me!"

Gabriel grinned. "I was hardly silent."

"Lies."

"I was not," he protested.

"You have an uncanny ability to sneak," she told him, twisting back around to stare out of the window again. "What if they get caught in the snow? The roads are awful this year."

"They only have a short distance to travel, Millie. Cease fretting."

She rolled her eyes to herself. "Oh yes that will do it, dear husband. Now I am miraculously cured of all my worries. All I should have done was cease fretting."

He used his hands upon her shoulders to urge her to face him again and she couldn't help but let her frown soften when he cupped her face and pressed a gentle kiss to her nose. She wasn't certain she would ever get used to the gentleness with which this man could handle her. She saw the way in which her husband was viewed at times—nothing more than a scarred hulk of a man—but they did not know the tenderness and caring that lay in his heart.

She did. More than ever now. After nearly eight months of marriage, they were finding their feet. Becoming a viscountess had not been easy and trying to find a way to fulfil her ambitions for the shop and become a member of high society had been a compromise, but one she was willing to make.

Only for Gabriel, though.

Thankfully they didn't need acceptance from Society—Gabriel had long since washed his hands of them and they had their friends who remained loyal. Though she did not spend every day at the shop any longer, she remained heavily involved and in some ways, she was grateful for that. Years of striving had left her with little time to enjoy everything life had to offer.

"Your mother made it through the snow as did

Emma and Lydia. They shall make it," Gabriel reminded her.

A giggle from the parlor room reminded Millie she was neglecting their current guests. Decked in fresh greenery and filled with the scent of her mother's stewed pudding, the huge house finally felt like home during the festive period. It would be even more so soon if the rest of their guests arrived.

"Look," Gabriel says, "that looks like the Earl of Henleigh's carriage."

"Oh good." She twisted to spy a dark carriage carving through the snow and allowed herself a long breath. "With any luck, the rest of them shall be here shortly."

"Come, we had better get ready to greet them." He laced his fingers between hers and she glanced at their joined hands. Her fingers no longer held the roughness of a working woman but she kept them busy enough these days, knitting garments for those less privileged and offering as much work as she could from her shop. With any luck, the lease on her newest shop would be completed by January and they could expand and hire even more people.

"Wait," she said, tugging his hand.

He scowled. "Is something the matter?"

She shook her head and smiled. "No, of course not. It's just...well, we will not have much time alone together this Christmas and I wanted to thank you."

"Thank me?"

"I know it has not been easy and I am no typical viscountess—"

"Millie—"

She held up a hand. "But I could not ask for a more patient, loving husband." She gestured about the house. "This is not the life I expected for myself, but I love it." She swallowed the knot building in her throat. "And I love you."

A slow smile curved his lips and her heart gave a little stutter, making her head swim.

"I am not a typical viscount in case you have forgotten."

Millie sketched a finger over his lip, tracing the smile that came so frequently these days. "Well, you are a barbarian..." she teased.

"I think from the moment I kidnapped you and you hurled insults at me, I knew nothing would ever be easy with you," he continued. "I do not want easy, though. I want you. I want to strive and fight for what's best for us and those we love."

"Me too." She rose on her toes and pressed a kiss to his lips.

The bell rang through the house and they eased apart. She could not wait to see all of the Kidnap Club members but she was going to miss having her husband to herself.

"Looks like the others made it too." Gabriel nodded toward the window and Millie spied two more carriages making their way up the road.

"Oh good. I would hate all of the planning to go

to waste."

"Yes, and all my excellent pudding-making skills."

"Would we say excellent?"

Gabriel narrowed his gaze at her. "Your mother said it was better than yours."

"My mother is a traitor."

They moved passed the parlor room where Lydia played with dolls on the floor with Millie's mother. Emma briefly met Millie's gaze and they shared a smile. Since Westwick had been forced to flee to Europe thanks to mounting debts that even a duke could not pay and his man being arrested and tried for several criminal acts thanks to an anonymous article in a newspaper that just so happened to be owned by the Earl of Henleigh, there had been a change in Gabriel's sister. She was even writing to a lovely young man who she had no doubt would be wonderful for Emma.

She came to Gabriel's side as Guy and Freya made their way up the steps toward the house, their cheeks rosy and clothes flecked in snow. Gabriel looped his fingers between hers and gripped her hand tight, sending an affectionate look her way. Warmth spread through her, reaching straight to her heart.

"Did I ever tell you I'm glad you kidnapped me?" she asked.

He grinned. "Never."

"Liar."

"You can tell me again."

"Later," she promised. "Much later."

THE END

ABOUT THE AUTHOR

Samantha Holt

USA TODAY Bestselling Author Samantha Holt is known for fun, witty, and usually steamy historical romances. She's been a full-time writer for longer than she ever thought possible having originally trained as a nurse and an archaeologist. She's a champion napper, owner of too many animals, mum to twins, and lives in a small village near the very middle of England.

She's usually writing (or napping) but when she's not, Samantha is plotting (books of course!) with her husband, drinking coffee, climbing hills that are far too high for her fitness levels or visiting stately homes and pretending she's posh.

Find Samantha on her website www.samanthaholtromance.com

BOOKS IN THIS SERIES

The Kidnap Club

Capturing The Bride

She'll do anything to escape her betrothed. Even if she has to plot her own kidnapping…

Grace Beaumont is desperate. Set to be forced into an arranged marriage to a depraved man, she's out of options. Calling on The Kidnap Club—an elusive group of men who specialize in helping women escape difficult situations—is her last resort. She never thought she'd end up hopelessly attracted to the rake who kidnaps her. And yet…she is…

Lord Nash Fitzroy doesn't get emotionally attached. To anyone. He especially doesn't get attached to the women he rescues. He's a protector, a defender, and an occasional shoulder to cry on. That's all. But the longer he spends in the quick-witted Grace's company, the more he finds himself struggling to maintain the professional distance he needs to do his job—and protect his heart...

She's in trouble. He's a rake with troubles of his own. They weren't looking for love. But what will Grace and Nash do when it finds them?

Stealing The Heiress

She craved adventure...

Lady Rosamunde Stanley just never expected in the form of a kidnapping.

Well, an almost-kidnapping. The dastardly man only went and took the wrong woman!

But she soon discovers the dark, handsome man is not quite the terrible rogue she thinks him to be and she decides to put his experience to use. Can she persuade Russell to help her?

Russell might have kidnapped her, but he has no intention of keeping her. Even if the heat between them is driving him out of his wits and her crazy family makes him long for things a battle-hardened orphan like him should never want.

Their societal divide isn't the only reason to keep

his distance. Rosamunde is a bloody knife-carrying, picklock-wielding madwoman.

A far too appealing madwoman...

Taking The Spinster

The Earl of Henleigh has no time or desire for women. Well, that's a lie. He has the desire but since his disastrous engagement, he's avoided the opposite sex at all costs.

It's a shame Miss Haversham has not received the message, though.

The determined reporter refuses to leave Guy alone, convinced he's the key to a story. He might well be, but he'll be damned if she gets anywhere near his kidnap club.

Or his bed...

No woman has ever wanted that from him, and she'll be no different.

Freya Haversham wants one thing from the dark, wickedly handsome Earl of Henleigh.

Answers.

But the blasted man refuses to play nice. The story of these disappearing noble women could make her career and mean she doesn't have to write insipid gossip columns anymore, not to mention she might earn enough money to look after her elderly parents.

She's convinced he knows something, but he evades her at every turn.

That is, until he's kissing her until she's breathless. And rescuing her dog. Oh yes and looking after her mother. Could this heroic earl really be involved in something so awful as kidnapping and killing rich women?

Very well, perhaps he's playing too nice.

She can't let herself be distracted from this story, no matter how tempted she might be to give into the pull between them.